P9-AFO-621

TRAPPED!

The two riders came moving in slowly. Reese was on the hill above, so I had five men against me now, five men and a woman as deadly as any one of them.

Lying still on the sun-hot slope, I calculated my chances. Right now it was ten thousand to one they would kill me within the hour. Yet no man dies willingly, and there was in me a fierce desire to live, and not only to live, but to <u>win</u>!

Books by Louis L'Amour

Published by Bantam Books

Louis L'Amour
The Broken Gun

BANTAM BOOKS · TORONTO · NEW YORK · LONDON

To Alan Ladd
and Bill Bendix . . .
together again.

THE BROKEN GUN
A Bantam Book / published January 1966

All rights reserved.
Copyright © 1966 by Bantam Books, Inc.
This book may not be reproduced in whole or in part, by
mimeograph or any other means, without permission
in writing.

Published simultaneously in the United States and Canada

Bantam Books are published by Bantam Books, Inc., a subsidiary
of Grosset & Dunlap, Inc. Its trademark, consisting of the words
"Bantam Books" and the portrayal of a bantam, is registered in the
United States Patent Office and in other countries. Marca Registrada.
Bantam Books, Inc., 271 Madison Avenue, New York, N. Y. 10016.

PRINTED IN THE UNITED STATES OF AMERICA

Chapter 1 ~~~~~~~~~~~~~~~~~~~~~~~~~~~~~

He lay sprawled upon the concrete pavement of the alley in the darkening stain of his own blood, a man I had never seen before, a man with the face of an Apache warrior, struck down from behind and stabbed repeatedly in the back as he lay there.

Two police cars with flashing lights stood nearby, and a dozen shirt-sleeved or uniformed men stood about, waiting for the ambulance to come. But it was much too late for an ambulance.

"Sorry to get you out of bed at this time of night, Mr. Sheridan."

Detective Sergeant Tom Riley had introduced himself at the door of my motel room a few minutes before. He spoke politely, but I had a feeling he could not have cared less about awakening me. He was a man doing a hard, unpleasant job in the best way he knew how, and my own hunch was that he was pretty good at it.

"We thought you might know something about him."

Riley showed me the newspaper clipping and I recognized it as one that had appeared in the local paper the previous morning. It mentioned the fact that I, Dan Sheridan, author of a dozen volumes of western fiction and history, was in the city doing research.

What it neglected to mention was the slip I'd made during a moment of exuberance on a television interview when I said, "Among other things I want to find out what happened to the Toomey brothers."

The interviewer, with less alertness than usual with his kind, ignored the remark and went on to other things.

1

As a matter of fact, I had planned to keep the mystery of the vanishing Toomeys as my own private story, to be developed by me in my own good time.

The Toomeys had left Texas for Arizona some ninety years before, and up to a point their drive could be documented; beyond that point there was a complete void. Four thousand head of cattle and twenty-seven men had stepped right off into nothingness . . . or so it seemed.

"I can't be of much help, Sergeant," I said. "I never saw the man before."

"It was an outside chance." Riley was still looking at the body. "Can you think of any reason why he might have wanted to contact you?"

"Sure. I hear from all sorts of people. Some of them just want to talk about a story I've written, but most of them want help with a book they're writing themselves. Once in a blue moon somebody comes up with something I can use in a story."

"The name Alvarez means nothing to you?"

"No, it doesn't. Sorry."

That should have been the end of it, and all I could think of was getting back into bed. I'd had a busy day and a long flight, and I was tired.

Only it was not that simple. As I walked past the window of the motel office the clerk tapped on the glass and I went in. "Some calls for you, Mr. Sheridan. I didn't see you come in earlier."

He handed me a small sheaf of papers. A telegram from my publisher reminding me of our appointment in Beverly Hills, just ten days away. A telephone call from a newspaper woman who wished to do a feature story on me. The last was a scrawled message in an unfamiliar hand:

I have informations. I will come at one o'clock a.m.
                        Manuel Alvarez

I walked back outside. Riley was just getting into a

police car, but he stopped when I called. He glanced at the message, and listened to my explanation.

"Why one o'clock in the morning?" he said.

"You've got me. As I said, I never heard of the man. Not that it matters. In my business we meet all kinds."

"Mind if I keep this?"

"Go ahead." Then my curiosity got the better of me. "Sergeant, if you know anything about the man, please tell me. Something might ring a bell."

He considered that for a moment, then said, "He was the only honest one of a very disreputable family. His brothers have been in trouble of one kind or another since they were youngsters."

Nothing came of our talk, and I went back to bed. Morning came too soon. My first appointment was for nine o'clock, and while I waited for a cab I bought a newspaper.

The item was on the inside of the front page and gave only the bare facts of the story. Yet there was one difference, a difference that began with the headline:

SECOND BROTHER SLAIN IN TWO WEEKS

Pete Alvarez had been shot to death by a deputy sheriff while attempting to escape arrest for stealing cattle.

There was one more thing. The final paragraph stated: *The brothers are survived by a third, Pio Alvarez, of the same address.* It added the fact that Pio Alvarez had recently been released from prison.

Pio? Pio Alvarez? *Sergeant* Pio Alvarez?

Unknowingly, then, I had given Riley false information. It was true that I knew nothing of Manuel Alvarez, but I knew a great deal about Pio.

We had served in the same battalion in Korea, where Pio had been court-martialed three times, suffered company punishment too many times to remember, but had proved a first-class fighting man. We had been wounded within hours of each other, been captured at the same time, and together we had escaped. We had fought to-

3

gether in Korea, and having watched him operate, I was glad of it.

Two-thirds of the blood in his veins, he told me proudly, was Apache. One-third was Spanish-Yaqui, from Sonora.

By blood and inclination he knew only one way to fight, and he fought to win. During the long trek of our escape he had chances to fight, and we survived. With any other man than Pio I might not have made it.

My first thought on seeing that article was to reach for a dime and call him. My second was simply to forget it.

Pio and I had fought side by side. We had slept in the rain, hiked through the snow, hunted cover and warmth like wild animals; but that was past, and we lived now in another world. Pio had always been a trouble-maker and I had no reason to believe he had changed. The chances were good that Manuel, hearing that I was in town and knowing I had been a friend to Pio, had come to me for aid in getting Pio out of trouble.

We had shared much together in the past, but he had chosen to live outside the law, and I had taken another route that lay well within the lines of public responsibility.

My morning's work at the Historical Society came to nothing. The files of the earliest newspapers held no mention of either Clyde or John Toomey, nor was there a brand registered in either name.

Cattle ranching in Arizona had only just begun when the Toomey brothers arrived. In 1864, a man named Stevens held a few cattle in a valley close to Prescott, and Osborn and Ehle had driven a few hundred head into Yavapai County a year or two later. Stevens managed to hold his cattle by guarding them night and day, but Osborn and Ehle had theirs stampeded by Indians, and lost them all. Henry C. Hooker had been the first real cattleman in the Territory, driving in several herds for sale to the army, and finally had settled with one of them in the Sulphur Springs Valley. That was in 1872.

There was a good deal of information in the old records and newspapers, as well as in Hinton, Lockwood, and others, but no mention of the Toomeys.

At the land office I drew another blank. There was no record of any claims or deeds in the Toomey name, but it was there I saw the fat man for the third time.

He had been reading a newspaper in the lobby of the motel when I picked up my mail, and he had been standing on the curb when I left the Historical Society. Now he was here, chatting with a man in the land office.

It could be coincidence, but I was not prepared to believe that. He could also be a police detective, but I found that hard to believe too.

The only clue Riley had seemed to have in the investigation of the Alvarez killing was the clipping about me and the note Alvarez had left, so it was possible Riley might be having me followed. However, this man had the appearance of a successful businessman, or perhaps a cattleman.

Was he actually following me? For a moment I had an impulse to walk over and ask him, but he had only to deny it to make me look the fool. So I chose the better course, called a cab, and went to a popular cocktail lounge and ordered a drink. Within five minutes he was seated at a table not far from me with a drink of his own.

The hell with it. This looked like trouble, and the last thing I wanted was to get mixed up in something that was no concern of mine. I would buy a ticket for Los Angeles on the evening plane . . . or the next one out.

But by the time my drink was finished the fat man had visited a phone booth, and had also spoken to several people who came into the bar or passed through, and he seemed to be well known to them all.

As I was about to get up from the table a tall man wearing a white western-style hat came into the bar, glanced my way, and came over. He pulled out a chair and sat down.

"Dan Sheridan? I'm Colin Wells . . . own the Strawb'ry outfit over east of here. One of the biggest in the

5

state. When I heard you, a western writer, were in town I decided the least I could do was show some western hospitality. Figured I'd hunt you up an' invite you out to the place. Give you a chance to see what western ranch life is like these days."

He was a big, genial man, and the offer was not unusual. We talked for several minutes about ranching, modern style. Leading him on by discreet questions, I soon had a fairly clear idea of the Wells outfit, the cattle they ran, and conditions generally. And I managed to do this without revealing my own background.

"You ought to get out on the range and get the feel of it. We've got a right nice little place out there, and a pool if you like to swim. You come any time you're of a mind to, and stay as long as you like."

"Where is your place?"

"Over on the Verde . . . that's a river." He paused. "My foreman's in town with the station wagon. Drive you right out there if you want to go."

John Toomey had mentioned the Verde. It was to the valley of the Verde that he had come after that long, dusty drive from Texas.

It was a heaven-sent opportunity to look over the terrain where the Toomeys had settled, and there might even be some clue as to what took place after their arrival, although I knew that after ninety years the chance of that was slight.

But it would get me out of town and away from any further developments in the Alvarez killing. I had nothing to do with it—and I wanted nothing to do with it.

With luck I could look over the terrain, revive my knowledge of that area, and return to town, catch a plane and be in Los Angeles within a matter of forty-eight hours or so.

It looked like a good plan, and if the fat lad over there at the other table wanted to follow me into the mountains, he was welcome to do so.

A good plan . . . only as with so many such plans, there was a joker in the deck.

Chapter 2 ᴧᴧᴧᴧᴧᴧᴧᴧᴧᴧᴧᴧᴧᴧᴧᴧᴧᴧᴧᴧᴧᴧᴧᴧ

When the station wagon reached the top of the pass the driver pulled off the road. He was a tall, loose-jointed man with a lantern jaw and piercing eyes of cold gray. He wore badly scuffed boots, blue jeans, and a shirt of a nondescript grayish color. Pushing his hat back on his narrow skull, he indicated the broad sweep of land that lay before us.

"There lies the Strawb'y. Runs clean to the river."

From my study of aerial photographs, I recognized the two peaks off to the northeast as Squaw Peak and Cedar Bench, neither nearly so imposing as the Four Peaks of the Mazatzals off to the southeast.

"It's big, all right. There must be a hundred thousand acres in there."

"For a greenhorn," the driver admitted grudgingly, "you're a fair judge of country. She'll run a hundred and twenty thousand, and Bent Seward's place is almost as big."

I pointed to a far-off cluster of roofs, glinting in the sunlight. "What's that?"

"The Bar-Bell—Seward's place. They're kinfolk."

To a man pushing a trail herd with more than fifteen hundred miles behind it, this country must have looked like paradise itself.

Such a drive needed men with hair on their chests, men willing to gamble life and limb against thirst, distance, and wandering war parties of Apaches. Only unseasonal rains could have gotten them through, but I had the few pages in John Toomey's own hand to prove that they did get through.

And beyond that . . . *nothing*.

"Always like to show the place," the driver commented

as he swung the car back into the road. "She's a fair piece of country."

We had started down the long, winding hill road before I asked my question. "Where's Lost River from here?"

The driver's head turned sharply. "Lost River? Where'd you ever hear of that?"

"Down around Phoenix, I think. Yes, it was Phoenix. Some old fellow in the hotel lobby. He heard me talking about coming up this way, and mentioned it. Said it was the best water anywhere around." I was lying, and I hoped lying smoothly. "Said he used to punch cows up this way."

The driver was irritated. "Must've been a mighty old man. There's not many know Lost River, and that water hasn't been important for years. Not since we drilled all those wells."

"Must be pretty wild over there."

"It is. Ain't changed a mite in fifty, sixty years. I work this range all the time, and I haven't been over there since year before last." He looked off toward where Lost River must lie. "Only three or four times in the past five years," he added.

It was hot. Looking through the shimmering heat waves at the far-off mountains, I found myself wishing for a long cool drink and a cold shower. The mountains were gathering blue mist in the hollows and canyons.

Suddenly I was uneasy. Why had I come away out here? What kind of a fool was I to start tracing down some ninety-year-old mystery when there were stories to be done with less trouble? And suppose there was no mystery at all?

My eyes turned in the direction of Lost River. Why did I believe that the answer lay over there?

My uneasiness would not leave me. Was it a result of that unfortunate killing in town? Or was it that sharp look the driver had given me when I mentioned Lost River?

It had all begun in New Orleans when I bought a

8

broken Bisley Colt in a second-hand store. Stuffed into the barrel, which nobody had attempted to clean, were some pages torn from a notebook or diary. They were rolled tightly, and had stayed hidden in the gun barrel.

Those pages were a strange document. Why these particular pages? Why were they hidden as they were? The gun was broken, so nobody would try to fire it, and whoever had hidden the pages must have hidden them in a hurry, in fear of being searched.

The mystery was compounded by the disappearance of John and Clyde Toomey. After driving four thousand head of cattle into the country, twenty-seven men had simply dropped off the edge of the world.

John Toomey had been no writer, but there was a consciousness of destiny in the man, and even a vein of poetry. He was aware that there might not always be such cattle drives, and he wanted to record his for whoever might read.

I might have dismissed the thing as a hoax but for the little points of fact and incident that could not have been known by anyone who was not present . . . or by a skilled researcher. They were the things a hoaxer would not think of, and they were evidence of authenticity to me.

The Texas end checked out easily. The Toomey family records were complete right up to the day of their departure. There were deeds, wills, jury and coroner's records. Old-timers recalled stories about the family and the tough Toomey boys.

There had been four brothers. The oldest had been killed fighting for the Confederacy. Clyde and John had gone north to fight for the Union because they believed in the country, and returned to find themselves objects of hatred. It was this that caused them to sell out and leave Texas.

Theirs had been an active, prosperous, and prominent family, important to the community in which they lived. They were definitely not the sort of men to be overlooked, wherever they might be, and they were sure to leave their mark upon the land.

Yet they had vanished. There were no records of them that I could find in Arizona.

"How much further?" I asked the driver.

"Five, six miles. You a friend of Colin's?"

"I'm a writer. Colin Wells heard I was in town and invited me out. It gives me a chance to get the feel of the country."

"Likes folks around, Colin does. . . . What sort of writin' you do?"

"Frontier background, mostly. Some western history."

"This here was Indian country. Apaches, mostly."

"I didn't get your name."

"Name's Reese . . . Floyd Reese."

It gave me an odd turn. In that cattle drive ninety years ago there had been a man named Reese. Not one of the originals, but a man picked up on the way. Until they reached the Pecos Valley there had been forty men with the herd; actually it was two herds, about equal in size. A dozen of the riders had come along only for the drive to New Mexico, and they had turned off toward Santa Fe. By that time the herd was trail broken and easier to handle, but an extra hand was always convenient.

John Toomey had hired Reese, but with misgivings. The man was surely running from something, and he proved a troublemaker. This Reese might be a relative.

"Is this your home country?"

"My old man worked for Strawbr'y. I was born on the place."

Obviously the world began and ended on Strawberry range, as far as Floyd Reese was concerned. I had met several such men, had grown up with them, in fact.

It always irritated me that people would take it for granted, as they often did, that a man would write about something of which he knew nothing. Colin Wells had assumed that, being a writer, I knew nothing of ranch life.

I had grown up on a ranch in Wyoming. From the time I was old enough to sit a saddle I had punched cows, and in my teens I had drifted south during vacations to ride for an outfit in Colorado, and later had ridden for another in Montana. I'd put in a year working the mines and lumber camps before I enlisted to fight in Korea. Korea had lasted two years.

The landing at Inchon, the march north to the Yalu, when we had been assured we would be home in time for Christmas, and then the bitter retreat back down the peninsula when the Chinese, who we had been assured would not fight, decided to fight. Wounded, I'd struggled three days through the snow before the Chinese caught me. Believing I was in such bad shape that I was a safe prisoner, they guarded me poorly, and I was able to slip away. Recaptured by another outfit, I met Pio Alvarez and we escaped together, fighting and running and hiding all the way back to the American lines.

After a battle-field commission I'd returned to the States, went to a school for guerilla fighters, did a year of State-side duty, followed by a school for Military Intelligence.

That was followed by a year in Berlin and West Germany, and then I was shipped out to Saigon and guerilla warfare in the jungles of Vietnam. Wounded again, captured again, I escaped again. And that convinced me I'd stretched my luck too far, so I returned to civilian life and to writing.

The station wagon slowed and I saw two riders coming down from the slope of a hill, a dried-up old man with a wide but not pleasant grin, and a tough-looking rider of thirty-five or so. Both were armed.

As they rode up alongside, Reese stopped. "This here's the writer," he said. "Name's Sheridan."

He indicated the two men. "Dad Styles and Rip Parker. Been ridin' for Strawbr'y for years."

As the wagon rolled on, I commented, "They were armed."

"Sure. We run into rustlers sometimes, and it makes a long trip for the sheriff. He doesn't much like to be bothered, so I hold a dep'ty's badge."

"Is rustling a problem?"

11

"You bet. They come out in trucks and hoss-trailers. They unload their horses, tear down a piece of fence and round up a few head of cattle. They load 'em into trucks and take off. They don't get far, usually. Not with us, they don't. The only road runs along or through our property for fifteen miles."

He turned to look at me, his eyes faintly taunting. "You been ridin' over Strawbr'y range for seven or eight miles now. Everything, anywhere you look, is Strawbr'y. Only way a man could get out of here unless we leave him go is to sprout wings."

"Do they ever make a fight of it? The rustlers, I mean?"

"Sure . . . who wants to get caught? They know what they got comin'."

The station wagon rolled up before the house and frankly, I was glad to get out. I did not like Floyd Reese, and I was glad to be free of him.

A Mexican in a white coat took my bag and typewriter from the back of the car as Colin Wells came down the steps with a drink in his hand. "Welcome to Strawbr'y! Come on in and have a drink. You're just in time to round up a few before supper!"

There was a girl standing on the steps, a dark-haired girl with gray eyes who wore beige slacks and blouse. She was looking at me with neither appraisal nor welcome. It was a startled look, I thought, and apprehensive as well.

"My sister-in-law, Sheridan, Belle Dawson," Colin said. "Belle, this is that writer you heard me speak of."

"How do you do." Her smile was quick and friendly. "A reader always enjoys meeting a writer."

"And vice versa," I said, smiling at her. "But don't be frightened. I'm not going to ask you if you have read anything of mine."

"Oh, but I have, Mr. Sheridan! All of them, I believe. You have a gift, a very real gift, for reconstructing the past."

"It isn't a gift. It's just a lot of hard, dusty work in

12

the files of old newspapers, in catalogues, diaries, coroners' reports, anything of the kind I can put my hands on."

My eyes swung away from hers, glimpsing a low, squat building of stone. It stood near the crest of a knoll about three hundred yards away, beyond the corrals. It was built of native stone and had no windows, only slits from which a rifle might be fired. Into my mind flashed words from John Toomey's journal: *"and on the second day we began building a fort, a place of refuge against attack by the Apache. It was a low, stone building that we finally completed, situated on a knoll near the spring."*

"Be careful, Mr. Sheridan," Belle said ironically. "Your curiosity is showing."

"That stone building out there reminded me of one back home. It startled me for a moment."

"It was on the place when Colin's grandfather settled here. They use it to store old harness, saddles, odds and ends of tools. It's a sort of catch-all, really."

Four thousand head of cattle and twenty-seven men, and it was to this place they had come.

"Bourbon, wasn't it?" Colin Wells came over, holding out a glass. "I've got a memory for drinks. Now if there's anything you want to know about the place, you ask Belle. She knows as much about it as I do."

Ninety years was a long time, and there was small possibility that I could find anything in the nature of a clue. That old building might be one of many such. The past was fresh in my mind because I had worked with it so much, and had been living it through all my books, and all the painstaking research that went into their writing.

"You will want to freshen up," Belle said abruptly. "Bring your drink and I'll show you to your room."

"Show him where the pool is, Belle. Chances are we'll all be out there when he comes out again. If you'd like a swim, Sheridan, climb into a suit and come on."

She led the way along a shadowed arcade that bordered the patio on three sides, passing the doors of several rooms, finally to stop opposite a fountain. Around the fountain were palm trees and flowers, keeping the patio green and cool.

"Right along and through the arch to the pool," Belle said, and I could see the glint of blue water through the opening.

"Thanks," I said, and she turned to leave, then hesitated.

"Mr. Sheridan," she said, keeping her voice low and deliberate, "if I were you I would make any excuse that comes to mind and leave as quickly as possible, and I mean tomorrow. Make any excuse—any at all—but leave. When you get back to town, if you are wise, you will leave Arizona."

"I'm afraid I don't understand."

"I have read your books, Mr. Sheridan. None of the others have. I may be a fool, and you will probably think me one, but don't stay in this house after tonight. And please do not repeat what I have said."

"My books are harmless enough."

"You're very thorough, Mr. Sheridan, and a book such as you may write can be dangerous. I do not know why you were invited here, but you must realize that there is little interest here in either books or writers . . . rather to the contrary. Colin does like guests, but he does not care for strangers. For some reason, Mr. Sheridan, you are very special."

"Colin Wells introduced you as his sister-in-law," I said.

"His brother was married to my sister."

"Was?"

"They were killed. They were killed last year in an accident when their car ran off a cliff over east of here."

"I'm sorry."

She walked away from me then, and I stood watching her go, a lovely girl, but a strange one.

Why had she taken enough interest to warn me? She was related to these people, in a sense at least. Was she a highly nervous, neurotic girl? I did not think so, not for a minute. She was a bright, intelligent girl, and not at all the type to be an alarmist.

Yet she had made a point. Why was I invited here? How did it happen that of all places I should be invited to the very place I wished to go? Did they hope that my being here might publicize the ranch so they might perhaps make a better sale? Were they celebrity collectors? Neither of these reasons seemed likely, and the uneasiness I had been feeling ever since being called to look at the body of Manuel Alvarez suddenly sharpened.

The room was spacious, cool, comfortable. As I undressed and showered I considered the situation. After all, this was what I had been looking for, and surely somebody here could tell me about the Toomeys. This was, I felt sure, the place they had elected to stay.

Only a few miles away was the Verde River, all the peaks mentioned as landmarks were nearby. This had to be the place.

Yet I had been advised to leave. Had the mystery of the vanishing brothers not been so far in the past I might have suspected a connection, but how could a ninety-year-old mystery possibly matter to anyone except someone as curious as myself?

But I was a man who preferred to avoid trouble, having seen enough of it in every way. I decided I would take a couple of rides around the country, but would arrange to leave very soon, as soon as I had scouted the terrain a little. I did want to see Lost River, and I wanted to be inside that old stone building for a few minutes at least. I had a hunch about that building, and if the hunch paid off, I might have the answer to many of my questions.

Irritating, nagging little suspicions kept coming to mind. After all, my training had been such as to make me notice, and I had noticed. Yet what did it all add up to?

Floyd Reese's odd expression when I mentioned Lost River . . . well, why not? It was a remote, unlikely place for a stranger to know about or ask about. His expression was natural.

The clerk in the land office? He had looked a bit startled when I asked about the Toomeys . . . more so than a man would who knew, as he maintained, nothing about them. He had handed me the T file and walked away, and a few minutes later, returning the file to its case, I had overheard him on the telephone.

I heard him say, "Yes, *Toomey*. That's right . . . *Toomey*."

And when I left the land office, the fat man was outside. He had been in the motel lobby and outside the Historical Society library before that. But he was probably a policeman, no matter how little he looked like it. He might be somebody from the D.A.'s office, checking up on me.

The hell with it. I was going to leave Arizona. It was a state I liked, a state I knew pretty well. It was, in fact, this very country through which I had ridden . . . how many years ago?

It had been twenty years ago, and with two others of my own age. We had been punching cows in Colorado and decided to drift back across country to the Colorado River, crossing at Needles.

The drink tasted good, and the shower felt even better. The view at the pool was breath-taking, and that did not mean the far-off hills, lighted by the fires of a setting sun. It was the immediate foreground that gripped the attention.

On the edge of the pool, beautifully tanned and wearing a white bikini, was Belle Dawson. Walking toward the diving board was a golden blonde in tune with a music all her own.

Beyond the pool was Colin Wells, seated at a table with a drink; with him was a short, stocky man who looked familiar.

It was the fat man from the hotel. Only he was not fat; at least, most of that solid, all too solid flesh was not fat. It was sheer brute strength, the strength of a man naturally powerful.

Colin must have said something, for the man turned

16

around. He was smoking a long black cigar, and even the cigar was familiar.

Belle turned to face me. "Oh? You're not swimming?" she said.

"The shower was what I wanted, and I wouldn't spoil the effect for anything. Although," I added, "I'm glad you're swimming."

"Do you mean me, or Doris?"

"The blonde girl? Yes, I'm glad she's swimming, too."

She was poised on the end of the diving board now, a position that allowed her to exhibit every aspect of her figure to best advantage.

A white-coated Mexican appeared beside me. "A drink, sir? May I get you something?"

"Vodka and tonic." The Mexican did not move, and I turned to look at him, wondering why he hesitated.

"*Si, señor*, vodka and tonic." There was more than acknowledgment of the request, there was respect and an unexpected friendliness in his eyes. "Thank you, sir."

"Colin will be disappointed," Belle said to me. "He's very proud of his pool, and he likes everybody to swim."

I did not like to swim among strangers. Even when there were no comments on the scars, I could see the curiosity they created, and I had not grown accustomed to it. They were so obviously bullet wounds.

"Colin likes everybody to take part in everything," Belle added.

Inadvertently I glanced at the girl on the diving board. "Everything?"

"That," Belle replied coolly, "is *Mrs.* Wells."

"A fortunate man, Mr. Wells."

With the undivided attention of everyone, Doris Wells dove, and a beautiful dive it was. Her lithe body slipped into the water like a knife into a sheath, and with no more sound. When she surfaced she swam to the side of the pool, and got out, and walked over to me.

"I'm Doris Wells. Excuse the wet hand. Colin forgot to tell me you were so handsome."

Belle saved me a reply. She also opened an escape

route. "Are you going to be with us long, Mr. Sheridan?"

"I can't stay, much as I should like it. I've been browsing around the country looking for an idea for a book, but I have a meeting shortly with my publisher in Los Angeles. I was thinking," he added, "of doing something on the Apache wars."

"Then by all means stay here." Doris pointed toward the horizon. "That peak over there is Turret Butte where Major Randall trapped some Apaches. There was quite a fight."

I knew the story. I even knew the date. It had been April 22, 1873. Randall had scaled the steep sides of the peak in the dark, and for once the Apaches were taken by surprise. It had been a brief but savage battle. Several Apaches had leaped over the almost sheer sides, to escape or die.

That fight and the one in the Salt River Canyon somewhat earlier had broken the back of Apache resistance in the Tonto. It was on the heels of that attack that John and Clyde Toomey had driven their cattle into the country.

The cattle, four thousand head, meant a packet of trouble. Until they reached the New Mexico country it had been easy to drive the two herds. After the extra hands left, it was difficult but not so bad as it had been early in the drive, for the herd was broken to the trail and easier to hold.

"I'd like to stay on, but my schedule won't permit it," I said.

I accepted my drink from the Mexican and followed Belle Dawson to a seat at a table near the pool. The view from the terrace looked toward the far-off mountains, the Four Peaks of the Mazatzals, and the ridges between.

"Why did you come here, anyway?" Belle asked.

I glanced at her and shrugged. "I wanted to get out of town. It's as simple as that. And I've always liked this part of the country. It was a chance to breathe some

18

mountain air, refresh myself on the Apache country . . . and then . . . well, I just wanted to get away.

"I suppose," I added, "Colin told you about the murder?"

"Murder?"

She was startled at the word, even more than she should have been, I thought.

"A man was killed outside my motel. His name was Alvarez."

She was very still, and then she said, "Pio?"

"Manuel . . . I don't think Pio would be so easy to kill."

She turned around to face me. "You *know* Pio Alvarez?"

"We were in the army together. He's what a western man would term 'salty,' very salty."

She looked about her quickly. Then she said, "Dan, don't even whisper that around here—that you know him, I mean. The name Alvarez isn't popular here."

"Manuel wasn't popular with somebody."

"I wasn't hinting, don't even imagine I was. I know nothing about Manuel, beyond recognizing him on the street, but Colin claimed the Alvarez brothers had been stealing his cattle for years."

"That detective in town—Tom Riley—he said Manuel was an honest man."

"Possibly. Colin didn't believe it, though. And they caught Pete Alvarez in the act."

It was my turn to be surprised. "Then it was here? Pete was killed *here?*"

"Of course. Floyd Reese killed him."

Chapter 3 ᵥᵥᵥᵥᵥᵥᵥᵥᵥᵥᵥᵥᵥᵥᵥᵥᵥᵥᵥᵥᵥᵥᵥᵥ

For several minutes I said nothing, for I was hurriedly taking stock. My trip to Arizona, planned to be brief and thorough, was suddenly developing into something resembling a nightmare.

A man had been killed who was seeking me; his youngest brother had also been killed, and on the very ranch where I was now a guest. The third brother, a very tough, dangerous man, would surely be somewhere around. Leaving town to escape any further involvement in the Alvarez affair, I had plunged myself right into the middle of it.

Belle Dawson was right, of course. The quicker I got out of here, and out of the state, the better for me and all concerned. As for the police, if they wanted me they would know where to find me. I was not exactly unknown.

Yet the question remained: Why had Colin Wells invited me out here in the first place?

An answer came to me, but I dismissed it as improbable and foolish. What bearing could a ninety-year-old disappearance have on the present situation?

The answer was obvious . . . nothing at all.

We sat there quietly, watching the swimmers, from time to time letting our eyes drift toward the faraway hills.

Whatever happened, I must be on my guard. That was not difficult for me, because I have never been what might be called a trusting man. Having lived alone under such odd circumstances as I had, I was friendly but wary. I know the wariness did not show, for I have frequently been called too trusting by people who knew me only slightly. It was their viewpoint and they were welcome to it, but the fact was that the reverse was the case.

"If you want to go in tomorrow, I'll drive you," she offered.

"Now there's incentive if I ever heard it. Of course, I'll go, and thanks for the offer. However, there are a couple of things I'd like cleared up."

"Such as?"

"You . . . you do not speak as if these people were your friends, yet everything seems to point to the idea that they are just that."

"I have a ranch on the Little Cougar." She gestured. "It's right over there."

Little Cougar . . . I knew it by reputation, a narrow canyon, quite deep, that ended in a valley . . . and right in the country where I wanted to ride.

"I don't want trouble, that's all." She spoke quietly. "If trouble starts here a lot of people are going to be hurt. As for Colin, I've known him since I was a child. I was born in town, but my folks lived on the ranch, and we spent a good deal of time there for a while, but for some reason I never understood we went there less and less. Finally, we went to Los Angeles to live. After my parents died I came back here, and in the meantime Sis married Aukie Wells."

"You stayed on, though?"

"No, I lived in New York and Los Angeles, and then after Sis and Aukie were killed I came back here. I've always loved the old place and wanted to build there, but Colin was against it."

"Any reason?"

"There was no good road in there, and it was lonely. He invited me to stay on here, and then made an offer for the place."

"You're planning to sell, then?"

She shrugged. "I don't want to, and yet common sense tells me I should. And to be honest, I have the feeling they'd like me away from here."

I looked at her in surprise. "I thought you were friends?"

21

"Not really. Although I don't know any reason why they should want me to go . . . unless . . . But that was a long time ago."

"What?" I insisted.

"Colin wanted to marry me."

Wells and the other man were walking around the pool toward us, and Belle said, "Colin had the pool put in two years ago. He likes the Olympic size, and he's really a very good swimmer."

As they stopped before us, Belle looked up. "I was just telling Mr. Sheridan about your swimming, Colin. I hadn't gotten as far as the medals."

He smiled deprecatingly, yet with obvious satisfaction. "Yes, I was pretty good," he commented, "and I can still swim. I like distance, though."

He turned toward his companion. "Sheridan, this is Mark Wilson, my cousin. He operates a car agency and rental outfit in town. But we're in a lot of deals together," he added.

Looking up, I met a pair of the coldest eyes I had ever seen, but eyes that also held a sort of casual contempt. It was an expression with which I was familiar. I had seen it first in the eyes of a Red Chinese officer to whom I was merely a thing to be questioned and then shot.

His handclasp was dead. He had thick, strong hands, but the clasp was the same as that I'd encountered in many fighters and wrestlers or other very powerful men, either subconsciously afraid of hurting, or so conscious of their strength they have no need to impress.

"How ya?" he said carelessly.

Then, ignoring me, he said to Colin, "I'm going down an' talk to Floyd." Looking past me, he leered at Belle. "See you, honey."

Belle's lips were tight and her eyes hard with anger, but a moment later her face had changed and she had relaxed.

Colin dropped into a chair beside the table. "If you

really want to see this country, Sheridan, you've got to ride. You ever been on a horse?"

"A few times."

"Good! We'll take us a ride then. Would six in the morning be too early? You city boys sleep late, I know."

"Six would be fine."

Colin got up. "See you at chow." He walked off, ignoring Belle.

"I had better get dressed," Belle said, but she did not move. Then she said, "Mr. Sheridan . . . Dan . . . can you ride? I mean, can you *really* ride?"

"I grew up on a ranch in Wyoming."

"Be careful."

When she had gone I sat watching the deepening shadows. There is no peace greater than that of twilight on the desert, but there was more to my waiting than a desire to watch the fading light. The time to study a land is when dawn or sunset lies upon it, with shadows to reveal every draw, hollow, or canyon. One can never know a desert land until one has seen it in those moments before and after sunset or sunrise. By day the glare of the sun erases the hollows and smooths out the terrain.

Out there was an answer to my problem, a problem suddenly important to others as well as to myself. There was a hint of some connection between the ninety-year-old mystery and the deaths of Pete and Manuel Alvarez. What the connection was I did not know, but I was now sure that it had some relation to my invitation to visit here.

But oddly, after I had been invited here, none of them showed any desire to talk to me, leaving me alone with Belle, who seemed almost as much an outsider as I.

Why the strange feeling of animosity? What was Belle warning me against? Why had the clerk at the land office immediately reported my request for information about the Toomeys?

Of course, this was the place. It had to be. The landmarks mentioned in the journal were here, the stone house was here, and somewhere within range of my vision, no doubt, the mystery of John and Clyde Toomey had been resolved.

What *had* happened here so long ago? Had all the riders been massacred by Apaches? There was no record of such an attack. Had some of their own riders turned on the Toomeys and killed them?

Two things I wanted here. To identify other spots mentioned in the journal, and if possible to locate the rest of that account.

Whatever happened here, must have happened suddenly, causing John Toomey to tear those sheets from the journal—perhaps awkward to hide in itself—and thrust them down the barrel of the broken gun.

Even now, with the little I had, I could write a fairly consistent account of that long trek across the country and of their arrival here. It might have been about like this, that first evening they spent here on the Verde.

Belle was right, of course. I should get away from here. No book was worth being involved in a murder, or what could easily become several murders. There were plenty of other books to be written.

While I sat there, the last canyons gave up their shadows to the night, and only the stars remained, and the dark, serrated rims of far-off mountains. Getting to my feet, I walked slowly back to my room.

The arcade was deep in shadow, for no lights had been turned on, and my room was dark. But as I opened the door I was immediately aware that I was not alone. Was it instinct? Or some subconscious perception of movement?

"No lights, señor." The voice was unfamiliar.

"I am a friend, señor, and I come from Pio."

"He is a good man, *amigo*."

"He said you would remember. He thinks much of you, señor. And there are not many whom he respects."

"What do you want, *amigo*?"

"To warn you, señor. They mean to kill you."

24

Suddenly something happened to me. Possibly it was the low voice in the dark room, but all at once I was thinking clearly again, thinking the way a man should who plays a dangerous game. This meeting in the dark brought things back, and I realized I had better continue to think clearly, to be constantly watchful. Or they would kill me, whoever *they* might be.

Suppose the room was bugged? Belle had known where I was to stay, so apparently it had been decided before I arrived. Who would bug it? I did not know, but the thing to do when in doubt was to act as if it were so.

Crossing the room to the unknown man, I took him by the arm. "Come!" I whispered. In the bathroom I turned on the water to drown other sound.

"The room may be bugged," I whispered; "they may be able to hear what we say there." I heard a sharp intake of breath. Since the coming of movies and television everyone knows about bugged rooms.

"Who is it I must fear?" I asked.

"All of them. You must fear them all! I was to warn you, señor, to get away quickly!"

"How did Pio know I was here?"

"He knows, señor, but I work on the ranch and it was my brother who served your drink, only I have no business at headquarters, and if I am found here I shall be suspected."

"One more thing. Do you know the name of Toomey?"

"Aaah? So that is it? I—"

There was a faint whisper of approaching footsteps and the man vanished like a ghost. For a moment a shadow showed in the bedroom door, and was gone. Then a shadow against the open window, and that was all.

Instantly I pushed a chair over and under cover of the sound I flicked the switch on my tape recorder. The door whipped open without warning, but as the lights went on I was calmly dictating.

"Marie," I was saying, "delete the last three lines and

25

mark the pages for a change from Spanish to Portuguese. That way I can use Macao. Get me a run-down on Macao as it is today, everything in current publications over the past few years.

"Particularly, anything dealing with Red China. You know the sort of thing I'll need. You should get my first tape by Monday, and I shall be flying in by the midde of the week. I have an appointment with Randall on Friday."

As I spoke I glanced over my shoulder. Colin Wells stood just inside the door, still gripping the knob in his left hand, the hardness in his eyes fading to doubt as he saw the tape recorder.

"Excuse me, Colin. You know how it is with writers. We never stop working. Others can leave their job at the office, but a writer carries it with him, buzzing around in his head wherever he goes. Am I late for dinner?"

Without waiting for a reply, I spoke into the mike. "I deleted the last bit of dialogue, Marie. Too melodramatic." After a momentary pause I added, "Murder is often very undramatic. At least, unannounced."

Colin's eyes swept the room, then he crossed to the bathroom, where he even pulled back the shower curtain.

"Is the maid taking care of you? We have to check on them, you know. I don't want my guests lacking anything, particularly towels."

Then almost as an afterthought, he said, "Yeah, supper's ready. I thought you'd forgotten. We eat earlier than folks do in town."

He went back to the door and, flicking off the recorder, I followed him.

The room was bugged, I felt sure now. Wells had been listening, and had come down on the rug hoping to catch whoever was warning me. He had almost succeeded. It was unlikely that he was fooled by the tape recorder, but he would be in doubt, for what I had said might well be true.

The dining room was bright with silver and crystal. We walked past the door and entered the playroom, a comfortable room with sofas and easy chairs, and at one end a pool table. Nearby a TV set was going, with nobody watching.

Doris glanced up, her expression enigmatic, her eyes flickering from me to Colin. "You have beautiful nights," I said to her; "it is no wonder you like living here."

Colin had started away, but he stopped and looked back. "My people built this place, Sheridan, built it from scratch, and we've reason to love it. Nobody is going to take it from us. I mean . . . *nobody!*"

Lacking anything else to say, I commented, "If you can keep the real estate people away, you should be all right."

Mark Wilson, talking to a big young man at the other end of the table, faced around. "What do you mean by that remark?"

Belle interrupted, ignoring him. "Real estate people in Arizona aren't as bad as in Los Angeles, Mr. Sheridan. Out there they seem to be trying to buy every empty piece of land for a subdivision."

"Dinner is on the table," Doris suggested. "If you boys can stop talking real estate, we can eat."

Belle got up at once. "You must be hungry," she said to me, "and I certainly am. Come on!"

As we reached the table, Belle turned. "You haven't met Colin's brother. This is Jimbo Wells. You may have heard of him. And this is Benton Seward, our closest neighbor."

Whatever else might be said of them, they ate well, and I am a man who appreciates good food. But as the evening wore on I began to wonder, and kept remembering the line so often printed in accounts of executions: "The condemned man ate a hearty meal."

The dress that Doris Wells wore was scarcely less revealing than the bikini, but it was not entirely her fault. Nature had provided her with equipment that defied concealment . . . and it was Doris who brought gaiety and laughter to the meal.

No doubt I contributed my share, for there is something in me, some nervous reaction, that is stirred to levity by the deeply serious or the dangerous. Tonight was no exception.

Without doubt they had me in a corner, but I had no idea what had brought it about. For some reason they were afraid of me, and their instinct, like that of some wild animals, was to kill whatever they feared. But for the first time I had a lead.

The sharp reaction to my idle comment about real estate brokers opened a door to speculation.

What was it they feared? Were they afraid I might stir up something to cloud the title of the Wells's holdings? Was that title somehow vulnerable?

If that was the case then I could understand their worry. This ranch and the adjoining property they held must be worth several millions.

Was there a connection between the killing of Manuel Alvarez and this ranch? Pete Alvarez had been killed here, by Floyd Reese—for rustling . . . or because he knew something that must not be told?

As we ate, one part of my mind kept worrying over the problem like a dog over a bone. Suppose the Toomey brothers had settled on this land and somehow been displaced by the Wells outfit? If the Wells family had never tried to sell any of their land perhaps there had never been a title search; and even if there had been, the methods of acquiring land in pioneer days had been irregular, to say the least.

From time to time my eyes wandered to Jimbo Wells. I knew of him, of course. He had been a runner-up for the All-America, had broken an inter-collegiate shot-put record, and had played three years of professional football. He was big, fast, and notoriously rough, even in such a rough game as pro football.

He had that close-cropped, freshly washed look so often

associated with bright young college football players and nice boys, but my recollection of his playing and of the gossip around the world of sports was that he was something less than a nice boy.

"We never had a writer on the place before." He was looking right at me, and I knew trouble when I saw it coming.

"You must have met a few at college."

"Panty-waists." Jimbo was deliberately contemptuous. "They had a few around, all right. I had nothing to do with them."

It was a comment to ignore, and I did, turning to exchange a comment with Belle.

For the first time in years I had suddenly wanted, really *wanted,* to throw a punch. I felt it rising in me, but my good sense rang a warning bell. I was on their property, far from possible intervention in case of trouble, and in a situation where I couldn't win without losing.

My first warning was the grating of his chair and the rattle of a dish as he pushed against it. Then he had grabbed me by the collar. "Now look, writer, that wasn't polite. I wasn't through talking to you."

"No?"

"You just tell me: I want to know how you writers work. Now supposin' you were going to do a story on this ranch, how would you go about it?"

My left hand lifted and I suddenly dug my thumb under the hand that held my collar and got hold of his little finger, bending it sharply back. He had to let go or have his finger broken, and he let go.

"Why, you—"

"You were asking how I'd work," I replied calmly. "In the first place, I doubt if there is a good story of my type concerning this ranch. As for stories of the Apaches, I had considered that, but they have been done and over-done, mostly by people who know little about the subject. No, I think I'd look elsewhere for a story."

Jimbo was mad clear through. He had been stopped,

29

and stopped at something he probably believed he could do better than anyone else. What I had done had required neither strength nor skill, and he knew it.

Eager as I was to take a punch at him, I knew the best thing I could do would be to get away from this ranch, and quickly. But how? I could scarcely walk out, and the only transportation would have to be provided by them. Would they refuse? I was sure, now, that they had no intention of letting me leave . . . unless they could decide that I was harmless.

My eyes had seen their faces while Jimbo held my collar. Colin had looked smug, and pleased. Doris was simply curious. She was not disturbed by what was happening at her dinner table, just curious to see what the two man-beasts might do to each other. Rather, at what Jimbo might do to me, for the idea that I might have a chance with him never, I was sure, entered her mind.

Doris, I thought, would have wanted a seat down front when the Christians were fed to the lions. She was the sort whom violence excited . . . pleasurably.

I had not seen Belle's face. Benton Seward had been alarmed, I thought. He impressed me as one who would not care what happened as long as he was not called upon to witness it, and as long as he was safely away with an alibi.

My anger was mounting. A good deal of it was because of my own foolishness in ever getting trapped in a place like this, but a lot of it was with them, so smug, so assured, so sure they could get away with whatever they chose to do. Suddenly I wanted to slap them right in the face with it.

I sat up a bit and leaned toward them. "As a matter of fact, if I planned a story on this ranch I'd first come here, ride around a bit, and then I'd dig into the history of it. Not the obvious stuff that everybody knows, but the forgotten stories, stories about the men who first drove cattle into this country, and what happened to them."

Belle's knee came hard against mine under the table,

and I knew it was a warning pressure. She wanted to stop me before I bought trouble. But I was mad, and in no mood to stop.

That beefy gorilla across the table had made me mad clear through. Had he grabbed me at that moment he would have got himself a fat lip or a broken nose, no matter what the consequences might be. I'd met a few of his kind in the lumber woods or mining camps, and I had never liked the type.

"The first comers were Mexicans or Spanish," I went on, "but the Texans were not far behind. I would find out about the first Texans who drove cattle into this country, and I'd ask questions, I'd dig for the old records, look into the old diaries. I would find out what happened to them."

Colin's cold, measuring eyes were on me, and all trace of his drinking was gone from them. "What do you think did happen, Sheridan?" he asked.

"Where there is wealth," I said, "there are always men who will kill to get it."

He looked hard at me, and he was not smiling. "And kill to keep it, Sheridan," he said.

Doris got up. "Let's go into the playroom," she suggested. "We can have some coffee and brandy there."

Every grain of common sense I had warned me to make any excuse to get away from there, but I was feeling stubborn. If they wanted trouble, they could have it.

Belle stayed seated beside me, her face a little pale, her eyes unnaturally large.

Doris had reached the bar. The Mexican in the white coat was there, his face impassive. "Brandy or a liqueur?" Colin said.

"Do you have Calvados?" I asked.

"We have it," Colin replied, too sharply. "Whatever you want, we've got it."

With an attempt at a diversion, I commented, "I'd been thinking of an article on the Indian remains—picture-writing, that sort of thing."

"It's been done," Colin replied irritably.

"They may have missed something."

Colin swirled his brandy, then looked up at me, his eyes coldly amused. "If you want to see picture-writing, and if you can ride well enough to stay in a saddle, I'll show you some of the best. We can ride over that way tomorrow." He smiled. "In fact, we'll show you the handwriting on the wall."

"I'd like that. As for staying in a saddle, I can give it a try." I got to my feet. "Now, if you will excuse me, I've had a long day, and after Riley woke me up I didn't get much sleep last night."

"That's right, city boy," Jimbo taunted. "You'll need all the sleep you can get."

Doris had turned her head and was looking directly at me. "You say Riley woke you up last night? Now, what Riley would that be?"

"Sergeant Riley. He was investigating a murder." I kept my face expressionless and my tone casual. "A man named Manuel Alvarez was murdered in the alley near my motel."

They were all looking at me now. Jimbo was no longer sneering. He looked belligerent, but scared too.

"Why would they want to question you?" Doris asked.

"They found a newspaper clipping in his pocket that mentioned my being in town, and he had tried to make an appointment with me. In fact, he made one, but was killed before he could keep it."

"Then you never talked to him?"

"No, I knew nothing about him." Suddenly I decided to buy myself a little insurance, slight though it might be. "I'm not sure Riley believed me. He told me to keep in touch, so I left him a note before coming out here."

I stifled a yawn. "Good night, everybody. It was a wonderful dinner."

Out on the terrace I looked at the night, inhaling deeply. The sky was alive with stars. Down at the corrals a horse stamped and blew through his nostrils.

Belle came out and stood beside me. "You're a fool,

Dan Sheridan, if you ride into those hills tomorrow. Colin means to kill you."

"Don't be silly."

"Make a wrong step on one of those trails and you can fall five hundred feet. There wouldn't even be an investigation."

"Are you kidding?"

"You're forgetting that Colin is a big wheel in this state. He contributes to both parties at election time, and he's well liked in important circles. He is also a deputy sheriff, empowered to investigate such accidents."

"Accidents?"

"What else? It will be a case of a greenhorn who couldn't handle a horse on a mountain trail. They will say a rabbit jumped, or a rattler scared your horse.

"After all," she added, "you are an invited guest. There will be no known motive. Who would investigate an obvious accident?"

Who, indeed?

"Riley . . . Riley would be curious," I said.

"Tom Riley—and I know him well—is a city officer who investigates city crimes. The chief of detectives is a poker-playing pal of Colin's, to whom Colin loses money occasionally. He has been a guest here himself, has slept in the very room you are sleeping in. Believe me, Tom Riley would have to present a very strong case before there would be any investigation of Colin.

"Besides," she went on, "you're not only beyond the city jurisdiction, you're in another county."

But there was one thing none of them considered. Such a man as Manuel Alvarez may go through life unnoticed and unimportant, but if he is murdered then suddenly he is the focus of attention. The newspapers, the officials—every cog in the enormous wheel of investigative officialdom goes to work.

Already the papers had mentioned the deaths of the two brothers, one of them having happened on this ranch. I doubted very much if another death on the same ranch could be quieted down. However, I was naturally reluctant to die to prove my point.

I would be careful. I would see Lost River, and I would get away. Or so I hoped.

Chapter 4

The ridges of that sun-baked land lie high and broken, and there are no easy paths. The best trails were made long, long ago, and not by Indians, but by Those Who Went Before . . . by the Old Ones.

Those earlier men made the trails, or followed those made by wild animals, and the Old Ones left their cairns, loose piles of stones left there one by one as an offering to the god of the trail or as a symbolic lightening of the burden. Such casual piles looked as if they had been raked together, like dried leaves, but each stone had been left by someone who had passed that way.

There is old magic in those stone piles. The Indians who came later realized this, and continued the practice; and occasionally a white man who respected the mountain gods did likewise.

Such piles of stone are found, too, on the high passes of Tibet, and in Mongolia. The idea is ancient; and the men who began it here first passed over these trails . . . how long ago?

Here and there some late-comer had dug into the piles looking for treasure, but there is no treasure to be found there except the treasure of wonder, and for that no man need dig . . . unless he digs within himself.

Wild horses, wandering cougars, or bighorn sheep know the piles. The buzzards leave no trails, but they know the rock piles too. High in the blue where the buzzards fly all trails are visible, and they share among themselves an ancient, secret knowledge of them. Where trails are, men may go; and where men go there is often death, and the buzzards have a pact with death.

The interest of the lone buzzard that flew above the basin that morning was casual, but where such parties rode there was a possibility, and buzzards exist upon possibilities. This one hung silent against the silent sky, and waited.

Floyd Reese was there—going along, he said, to care for the stock. He wore a belt gun and carried a rifle. A picnic lunch had been prepared, for this was to be an outing.

Reese took the trail first, with Colin Wells directly behind him. The hammer-headed bronc they led out for me looked like trouble, but I made a clumsy attempt to get in the saddle, doing so deliberately, for they were watching. Jimbo Wells turned away with a snort of disgust, but surprisingly, the horse stood still.

Belle rode just ahead of me, Jimbo close behind.

Nobody talked. It was clear and cool when we started, with the sun still low over the mountains in the east. Colin, I thought, was probably nursing a hang-over.

The trail we took led immediately into rough country, and I rode with care, studying my mount, and wondering what to expect from him. On every ranch there is at least one bad horse, and often several with peculiar quirks all their own. It has been a standard joke to provide a bad horse for a tenderfoot visitor, and the horse I rode certainly looked unprepossessing. I had expected a bucker, but he had seemed most docile. Nevertheless, there had to be a catch somewhere.

Obviously, the easiest way to kill me, if that was what they really wanted, was to get it done by a bad horse. In that case nothing could ever be proved, and the most of which they could be accused would be bad judgment in giving such a horse to a stranger.

The bronc walked along easily enough, although once, when skirting a wash where the bank was steep, he shied a little from the edge, and that set me thinking. Suppose the horse hated heights? And suppose we rode out upon one of those eyebrow, cliff-hanging trails?

The trail, following the contour of the land, wound steeply upward, reaching toward the top of the mesa. The bronc I was riding had so far shown no real itch for trouble, but I was a skeptic, and I kept remembering that shyness for even a small drop-off.

I was bothered, too, by the fact that Jimbo Wells was close behind me. Instinct warned me that if anyone was to do the rough stuff it would not be Colin. It would be Jimbo or Reese. The latter would not hesitate to do what he was told, and he would do it coldly and efficiently. Jimbo would do it out of pure delight . . . and it was obvious enough that he did not like me.

Belle's horse slowed, and she fell back beside me. The trail was narrow, but there was room for horses to double up. Doris, in fact, had pulled ahead to join Colin.

"Be careful," Belle warned softly. "Be very careful."

"How about you?"

"What do you mean?"

"Well, if something happens to me, you may be a witness. And as you say, you're not really a member of the family."

She was startled, and for a moment she made no response. "I don't think they would harm me," she said finally, but without any real assurance.

"Why do they want your place?" I asked her.

She shrugged. "I think they would like to own everything in the area. They have tried off and on for several years to buy it. They even tried to buy my sister's share."

"You owned it together?"

"Yes."

"What happened when she was killed? I mean to her share of it?"

"It reverted to me. That was the way grandad's will was written. If she had had children they would have inherited, but she had none."

36

We rode on then in silence. An idea had occurred to me that I hesitated to suggest, but finally I did. At least, I asked a question that was tantamount to a suggestion. "Did they know that? I mean, did the Wells family know about the will?"

"I didn't even realize it myself until they were settling her estate. And I am sure she herself didn't know."

Something had been disturbing me as we rode along, as something sometimes will that edges into the outer fringe of one's consciousness. Suddenly it came clearly to my attention.

There were horse tracks, fresh ones, that must have been made only a short time before we had come along. Here and there the tracks of the horses ahead of me in our group had wiped them out, but the earlier rider had kept his horse off the trail or on its very edge most of the time. He had ridden carefully, and several times he had stopped to look back. I could see the tracks where the horse had half turned, and there would be several tracks, as of an impatient horse dancing about, eager to be going on.

"Is this trail used often?" I asked.

"Almost never, I think. Unless somebody is riding to the Rincon or over into the New Mountains, they take the jeep trail that leads to my place on Cougar."

But I was almost sure that rider had ridden along the trail ahead of us earlier that morning. He had ridden that trail since dewfall, that much I knew.

Jimbo rode up beside us. "You two seem to be hittin' it off." He looked at me. "Won't do you no good," he said. "She's a cold babe. Won't do you no good at all."

I ignored the remark. "Are you working cattle up this way?" I asked.

"Nothin' but strays over here. We drift our stock over toward Shirt-tail this time of year. Grass is better over there. And up along the Verde bottoms."

So it was unlikely anybody from the ranch had come this way, unless it was somebody whose chief concern was to prepare for our arrival. I could not forget that Pio Alvarez was somewhere about, and if there was one thing I was sure about it was the mind of Pio Alvarez.

At least, I knew it in terms of violence, and I knew he was as cunning as a wild animal, and far more dangerous. Two of his brothers had been killed, at least one of them by a Strawberry rider. Unless I had forgotten all I had learned, Pio would be somewhere on Strawberry at this instant.

Benton Seward had left early to drive back to his own ranch, the Bar-Bell . . . or so he had said.

Where was Mark Wilson?

Suddenly I broke into a cold sweat. Slowly but surely, fear had been coming upon me. No matter what happened, I could expect no help. I was in this alone.

This ranch and the land for miles in any direction belonged to Colin and Jimbo Wells. This was their world. The men employed on the ranch were their men. I was an interloper, and would be considered so.

What they did not realize, I thought, was that my death would stir up more trouble than they could hope to quiet. I had too many connections, too many people knew of my ranch background, and any story of my accidental death would immediately arouse interest and bring demands for an investigation. This was something that I felt Colin had not grasped, for he was too filled with a sense of his own security, with confidence in his invulnerability.

But how much good was that going to do me?

Riding carefully, my eyes began to search out an escape route. Somehow or other I had to get away from them, and I must ride warily while thinking about it. If this horse I rode was dangerous on the high mountain paths, I must be ready to jump from the saddle at any time. So I rode with only my toes in the stirrups, every muscle alert for trouble.

We came down off the mesa by an easy trail, dropping into a small valley perhaps a mile in length and half that wide. I remembered from my study of aerial photos that there was a trail going out of this valley to the northwest, a trail that led back over the mountains toward Copper Creek.

That was a way out, and for a moment I fought the temptation to wheel my horse and take it on the run. I had never run from anything yet, but this time I'd let myself get boxed in, and I didn't like the feeling.

What about Belle? Would they dare attempt a move against her while I was free and able to talk?

Suddenly I felt like a fool. What was I getting in such a stew about? If my room had not been bugged, Colin certainly had showed up at a most inopportune time for me. They weren't people whom I could like, but what had actually happened? True, I had been warned by two people, but on what basis?

If I escaped at this moment, what could I report to a sheriff? Nothing that would stand up in court, or to which any officer was likely to listen. Yet all my reasoning did not do away with that body in the alley, the body of a man who had planned to meet me.

Was he killed to keep him from seeing me? And if so, why? What had he planned to say to me?

A thought occurred to me. Suppose that Pete Alvarez had known something that threatened the Wells family? He might have taunted them with it, letting them know for the first time that someone else knew about it.

Suppose that Manuel, with that same knowledge, planned to revenge his brother's death by bringing that knowledge to me, of whom he knew through his brother Pio?

Or was the danger to me because of my reference to the Toomey brothers during that TV interview?

Floyd Reese drew up sharply. "Something moved up there!" He spoke to Colin, but we all heard him, the small column having telescoped at the sudden halt.

"Coyote, probably . . . or a rabbit," said Colin.

"It was a man."

There was a low-voiced argument of which I heard one phrase only: ". . . couldn't be."

39

My horse was restless at our halting. He shifted nervously, but I made only a slight attempt to curb him, for if he should suddenly start to run I wanted it to seem accidental. In that way I might get a good start before anyone realized what I had in mind.

Then Floyd Reese led off again, only now he carried his rifle free of its scabbard.

The trail grew narrower. I rode half turned in the saddle, trying to watch both Reese and Jimbo. The latter saw my attitude and mistook it for fear. "Scared, city boy? Scared you'll fall? Hell, you wait until you see what's up ahead!"

I'd had a bellyful of Jimbo, so I gave it to him. "Hell," I said, "these mountains wouldn't make a patch on the San Juans of Colorado . . . or the Bighorns in Wyoming."

He started to speak, but I had the ball and kept it. "Up in Wyoming where I punched cows as a kid this country would pass for flat land."

He simply gawked at me—there was no other word for it. "You punched *cows?*"

"I was punching cattle when you wore pajamas with feet in them."

Belle was smiling, and I began to feel better. I'd had about enough of Junior.

The riders had stopped again, and were looking at something among the grass and rocks just off the trail, on a little bank, half facing toward us. Jimbo swung out and cantered up, anxious to talk to Colin, I thought, and I followed close so as not to give him a chance.

When I got there they were looking at an arrow made of stones. The earth clinging to some of the stones was still slightly damp—they had been plucked from their beds only a little while before.

Underneath the arrow was a sign with a word and a number: *Fox 38.*

"What the devil does that mean?" Colin demanded.

Nobody needed to tell me what it meant, but there was no need for me to tell them.

Reese was studying it, and finally he said, "You know

what that looks like, Mr. Wells? It looks like one of those army signs, pointing out a company or battalion area."

"There never was any army up here," Colin protested, "and that's a fresh sign."

I knew the sign was intended for me, and for me alone. Both Pio and I had been with Fox Company—F Company, if you will—of the 38th. It was a tough, fighting outfit that made a name for itself, and we had done some of that fighting before being moved as replacements to another company. Pio Alvarez knew I would read that sign for what it was; and where that arrow was he might be. Either that, or he was showing me this was my chance to get out, to get clear before it was too late.

It wasn't in me to let them rest easy. "If Reese is right, Colin," I said cheerfully, "you may be in trouble. If that stands for Fox Company of the 38th Infantry there's somebody around who was a first-class fighting man. They did a beautiful job in Korea."

They simply looked at me, not knowing what to make of it, but it gave Jimbo the chance he wanted. "This guy claims he used to punch cows!" he said. "I mean this writer here."

They didn't believe it. Their minds had formed a picture, and what Jimbo told them didn't fit into the frame they had accepted for me. Nor did it interest them very much, for they were wholly concerned with the fact that somebody unknown to them was obviously in the vicinity, and that interfered with their plans.

"That sign was probably made by the rider who came up the trail ahead of us," I commented. "But aren't we wasting a lot of time? I have to get back into town, and I'd like to see that Indian writing before it gets dark."

"It ain't far," Reese said, almost absently. He was looking in the direction in which the arrow pointed, trying to follow along with his mind, trying to see the trail ahead and where it might lead. "You go on, boss. I'm going to see where that arrow points."

41

"Let me go," I said. "Belle and I—we can ride out there a little way and see what we can find."

"You stay with us," Colin said curtly. "You could get in trouble out there." He hesitated, looking along the slope where Floyd Reese was riding. After a minute or two he swung his mount. "Come on," he said, and started on along the trail.

Half a mile farther along the trail started to dip down in a series of switch-backs to cross Little Cougar. On our right the massive escarpment of Cook's Mesa reared almost a thousand feet above us, and our trail mounted a spur. We had started up when from somewhere behind us there sounded a rifle shot, then another.

Jimbo swore, and Colin twisted in the saddle. Only Doris seemed cool. Suddenly I found myself watching her. She was listening, as calmly as she might have listened to some story told in her own living room.

"Colin!" Jimbo called. "Keep movin'! Let's get off the mountain!"

Reluctantly, it seemed, Colin went on. Belle was right ahead of me now, and only Jimbo was behind. My bronc was growing increasingly nervous, craning his neck away from the awesome drop that lay close at hand.

Belle turned in her saddle. "That's the Rincon." She pointed ahead.

I knew it was the Rincon. I knew all of this country from the aerial photos, but all I could think of then was the fact that there was a trail that cut off to the west from a spring a little way beyond the Rincon. It was a trail that might offer an escape, a route by which I might get out of these hills and away. No story was worth the trouble I might be getting into, or the death of any man, and I had a sneaking idea that Manuel Alvarez was dead because of me. Just how or why I did not know, but it all seemed to tie in together.

That point ahead, that would be Black Jack Point, beyond which the trail dropped down into the Rincon.

Rincon is a Spanish word meaning a corner, a nook, a

cozy place, a dwelling, or a remote place. Lost River lay near by, and Lost River was the last place mentioned by John Toomey in his diary.

Just at that moment I saw a deer. It was no more than a dozen yards off the trail . . . and then I saw another, and another. They moved unhurriedly away, an indication of the remoteness of the spot, if any were needed. Surely they had never been hunted or fired on.

Nobody commented on them. All conversation had suddenly stilled . . . rather, I had suddenly noticed it was quiet, but my consciousness told me that no word had been spoken for some time before the silence broke in upon me.

I looked around carefully. We were descending the trail now into the Rincon. Here the trail was wider. There were places where a man could make a run for it if he had to.

I felt the whip of the bullet an instant before I heard the crash of the report, and instinctively I kicked my feet free to roll from the saddle just as the bronc went up on his hind legs with a scream. I hit the dirt behind him, knees bent to take the shock, and instantly dove into the wiry brush alongside the trail, and just as swiftly moved from there.

And lay still.

Colin was swearing, and I heard Jimbo shout, *"Got him! Got him, Colin!"*

"Shut up, you fool!"

Colin wheeled his horse, turning on a dime, and came racing back along the trail toward the place where I had fallen. But Korea had been a good training ground and I was sixty feet from there by that time, using the watercourse that ran alongside the trail. Then I left it and wormed my way through the brush and up the steep slope. They were making enough noise to cover me, so I went fast.

Jimbo, his pistol out, was scouting the trail. From where I stopped to take stock of the situation I could see Doris sitting her horse calmly. In fact, she was shaking out a cigarette, no more disturbed than if they were hunting a snake or a wounded animal.

Belle had not moved. I think she knew now for certain that she too was marked to die. Once she made a move as if to turn, then stopped. And I could see the reason why.

The two riders I had met on the trail when I first drove to the ranch were there, blocking the way. She was trapped, as neatly boxed as I was, and both of us without a weapon.

Now they had us, and they meant to kill us. Reese had accepted the arrow and its sign as an excuse to leave the column; had it not been that, he would undoubtedly have found another reason. He had ridden on and planted himself to wait, and if he had killed me, or if they did, it would be put down to Pio Alvarez.

They had me and they had their scapegoat; and worst of all, they had Belle. For some reason they wanted her out of the way, too.

Chapter 5 ~~~~~~~~~~~~~~~~~~~~~~~~~~~~

It was preposterous. This was not the nineteenth century, the day of the rustler and the gun-fighter; this was the day of satellites and moon voyages. Yet here I was, trapped in a corner of western range country just as neatly as John and Clyde Toomey must have been trapped ninety years ago.

The two riders came moving in slowly. Reese was on the slope above, so I had five men against me now, five men and a woman who, I was sure, was as deadly as any one of them.

Lying still on the hot slope, I calculated my chances. Right now it seemed a thousand to one that they would kill me within the hour. But no man dies willingly, and there was in me a fierce desire to live—and not only to live, but to win.

Watching them, I pictured the slope behind me. It was thickly covered with cedar and a variety of desert growth, with some bunch grass too. Moreover, a little to my left and back of me there was a saddle about six or seven hundred feet higher than where I now lay. That provided my best chance.

Floyd Reese was up there somewhere, I knew, but down here in front of me were four men, all mounted. To escape, to live, I must go where those four could not follow unless they followed on foot. Nobody in his right mind would try to take a horse where I was going. Unarmed though I was, I felt I could give them a run for their money on foot, for I doubted whether any of them had devoted much time to clambering around in the mountains, and I had.

Backing away a few feet, I found a hollow. It was only a few inches below the level of the ground and extended for only a few feet, but I squirmed along it, used a boulder for cover, and angled back toward the saddle. There I made it to a cedar, and with substantial cover I stood up and managed to climb several feet before I had to drop to all fours. By that time I had another cedar behind me.

From the sounds down below, they were stringing out, ready to move in.

"You might as well come out." Colin spoke conversationally. "Pio won't try another shot."

From his tone he apparently believed me to be closer than I was, but the sound of his voice carried clearly. A few feet farther on, I reached an open spot where I would be without cover. Beyond that was a gash in the face of the mountain which, if I could reach it, would allow me to climb up for some distance well concealed.

"Maybe he's hurt," Colin said. "You sure he wasn't hit?"

"I don't see any blood." That was Jimbo speaking. "He was just scared. He still is."

"I don't believe he's scared," Doris said, "and if you stand there talking he'll get away."

Standing up, I walked right out onto the open space for five steps before I lost my nerve and dropped.

"Hey!" That was one of the riders from the road. "Something moved up there on the slope!"

The shirt I wore was olive-green wool, my slacks were slate gray. A man lying perfectly still on a mountain slope—or an animal, for that matter—is almost invisible. It is movement that draws the eye, and so I lay perfectly still.

"Might have been a bird—maybe a quail or a rabbit," Jimbo said.

"Go up there and find out," Colin said. "He can't be that far, but if something moved . . ."

"I might have been mistook," the cowhand said. "I see the wind movin' the cedars a mite."

There was nothing for it but to lie still. Right out in the open that way, a move now and I would be a target for more than one rifle.

The minutes edged by, and I heard no sound. "Hell," Jimbo said presently, "there's nothin' up there."

"Go look," Colin said, but he spoke less positively this time.

Now I heard movement, and after a long moment of indecision, I risked the chance of turning my head to one side so I could look downhill. My vision was obscured by grass and heavier growth, but I could see the two riders working along beside the trail, searching for me.

Belle Dawson chose that moment to move. She had been sitting her horse, almost forgotten. A known quantity, they were apparently not worried about her. They felt sure they had her there when they wanted her. Belle knew that, but it seemed that she might be trying to create a diversion for me. In any case, it worked.

She slapped the spurs to her horse and went down the trail at a dead run. Not back toward the ranch, but down trail toward the spring.

It was my chance and I took it, leaving the ground in a sprinter's start, and making for the cut in the mountainside in swift charging steps. Behind me yells sounded, but whether they had seen me or were all yelling at Belle, I did not know.

At the cut I slid to a stop and dropped to the edge. Then I turned around and lowered myself by my hands, feeling for a toe hold. I could find none and the bottom was fifteen feet down, so I took it half sliding, half falling.

Shaken, I hit bottom, but got up and swung around to start climbing. What had happened to Belle I had no idea, but I knew that for both our sakes I had to get away, and fast.

My condition was good, and I was wearing hiking boots rather than those usually worn for riding. I made a dozen fast steps, pulled myself over a waist-high dry waterfall, and began to climb. The cut took a small bend and this gave me added protection. I kept on climbing steadily.

Down below I could hear shouting and swearing. Pausing for breath after climbing a hundred yards or so, I glanced back. Jimbo was standing on the trail, his horse and mine close by. The others were not in sight. The shouts came from far down the trail.

I wondered how well Belle knew this country, but I knew she had lived part of her life on a ranch on the Cougar, and must have ridden over it many a time. She might know of a place to hide, and I hoped she did.

After a minute or so I went on climbing. Several times it was almost straight up, but each time I found footholds and was able to go on. I was within a dozen feet of the top when I heard a faint movement above me. I was caught in a bad place, but went on for a few steps before looking up.

Floyd Reese, rifle in hand, was seated at the point where the steep watercourse began, right on the lip of the mesa. His hat was tilted back, he held his rifle easily, and he was smiling. It was not a nice smile.

Stepping to a better foothold, and just a little closer, I looked up at him again. "Well," I said, "it looks like you got me."

"Dead to rights," he said. "I'm goin' to kill you, writer."

I met his look squarely. "Was it your grandfather who met the Toomeys when they crossed the Staked Plains?"

He was startled. "Now how in hell could you know *that?*"

The only weapon I had was bluff, and I didn't believe it would work. "John Toomey left a diary," I said, almost offhand. "Everybody knows that."

"Like the devil, they do."

"If you had done as much research as I have," I said, "you'd know all about it. Why, I know of two articles in the *Kansas Historical Quarterly* based on it.

"Toomey was writing home," I continued, "mailing pieces of it back so his folks in Texas would know about it." The lie was an easy one, for many pioneers had done just that. "Nobody ever tried to investigate what happened on this end, that's all."

I went on as casually as I could. "It wouldn't do you a bit of good to kill me. Everything I've found out about it is tape-recorded in Los Angeles. As soon as they started investigating my death or settling my estate they would play those tapes. After that you boys wouldn't have a chance."

About half of this was true, but he wasn't buying it. "Won't do you no good," he said. "You'll be dead."

"Look at it this way," I said, and I dove for him.

He fired.

Something plucked at my shoulder, but I had lunged forward, throwing myself against the slant of the cliff as I grabbed for him. He hadn't time to depress his aim enough, and my fingers caught at his pants leg.

Ever since learning judo in the army I had worked at it, and always kept in shape. When my fingers gripped the leg of his blue jeans, I jerked hard.

He slid off the rock and cannonaded into me and we

48

both rolled a dozen feet before bringing up hard on a ledge that was about a dozen feet across. He gripped his rifle and swung it at me, with a kind of half swing that caught me on the shoulder, and then I smashed into him. He was lean, tough, and mean.

Had he let go of the rifle he might have whipped me, but he tried to bring it up and I clipped him with a short left on the chin, then a right into the body, and stamped my foot down along his shin and drove my heel hard into his instep. He let out a grunt of pain and stepped back and I kicked him in the groin.

He fell and let go of the rifle. It flew a short arc through the air and went clattering among the rocks ten or twelve feet below.

Desperately, I wanted that rifle, but when I made a start for it, a bullet clipped rocks near me. Jimbo was down there, his rifle ready for another shot, and out in the open where I had to go he could scarcely miss.

My chest heaving from the exertion of the fight, I stepped back against the cliff. Reese gathered himself and came off the rocks. He was sick from that boot in the groin, but he was going to try. So I hit him again, and he went down to a sitting position. I took a swing at his face. He tried to duck, and my blow glanced off his cheek-bone, but he went down. His pistol was gone from the holster and there was no time to look for it, so I ripped the hunting knife and scabbard from his belt and shoved them behind my waistband.

Whipping around, I scrambled back up the cliff. As I went over the edge of the mesa I looked back. Reese was on his hands and knees, looking for his gun.

There might be a horse trail here on the mesa, so I wasted no time. Taking a route that led southwest which should eventually take me to the trail along New River, I started to run. Running fifty steps and walking fifty, I had covered half a mile and was running out of wind when glancing back, I saw a rider. A strange rider on a mouse-colored horse.

He was some distance off, but coming toward me. I

looked around the other way, and saw another. This one was Dad Styles, who had come up behind me. Sunlight gleamed on a rifle barrel, and I started to run again.

There was no shot.

They were closing in on me, gaining a little. As I ran I dipped into a hollow where there was a dry watercourse going off to the left, and I took it.

In spite of the bad footing I ran even harder. Once I fell. For a moment I lay there gasping. Then, slowly, I pulled myself up, and when I started on again it was at a walk. No horse was going to follow me from now on.

The dry watercourse ended abruptly in a fifty-foot drop, which was a waterfall after a rain. At one side I thought I saw a possible way down, though most of the rock was water-worn and smooth. Every step down would be a risk.

Somewhere I heard a hoof click on stone. It was unlikely they could get to me here, but I could not chance it.

Dropping to my knees, I lowered myself over the edge. I clung with my fingers and felt with an exploring toe for the tiny ledge I had seen from above. If I should fall now, it was unlikely anyone would ever find me in this remote, narrow canyon, scarcely more than a crack in the rocky edge of the mesa. Not even a coyote could get to me, and I would be left to the buzzards.

My toe found the ledge, tested it, and then balancing on the delicate edge, I moved one hand down a crack until the crack became narrow enough. Closing my fist to hold me there, I went down the face a little farther, finally swinging only by that closed fist. If I opened my hand, I would fall.

The fingers of my right hand found a grip, and then my toes found a hold, and bit by bit I eased on down the rocky face, and dropped when only a few feet above the bottom.

Here I was on a ledge of water-worn rock that was no more than twenty feet across and about that deep. Near the base of the cliff down which I had come there was a deep pool hollowed out by falling water, and the pool contained water now. There were a couple of feet of overhang near the pool, but no other shelter. There was no way they could come upon me except from the direction I had come, so now I went to the edge to look down. I drew back hurriedly.

The cliff fell away sheer for at least a hundred feet, and on that face there were no hand holds. Unless I could go back up again the way I had come down, there was no escape for me. I had trapped myself far better than they could have managed it, and it was probable that they knew it.

There was water, of course, but there was no food; and as for the way I had come, in that direction were the men who hunted me.

I made haste to get under the overhang, where I turned a rock on its side to get a comfortable flat surface, and sat down. From above I would be invisible.

There was no need to worry about the sun, for it would shine into this narrow canyon for not over an hour a day. What troubled me, besides my own plight, was that there was nothing I could do to help Belle. Though she had gotten away into the hills, she might need help.

Something moved on the rock above me, and I held myself back, careful to make no sound. Dust and a few pebbles fell over the lip.

"Sheridan?" It was Colin's voice. "You might as well answer. We know you're down there."

They suspected, with evidence enough, but they did not *know*, and what they did not know could hurt them. I held my silence, and waited.

Then suddenly, up there above me, I heard a hacking and pounding on the rock. Were they cutting footholds to come down? For a moment I was on the verge of looking out. The advantage was with me if anyone tried to come down that face, for while climbing down he would be helpless unless protected from above. Even in that case I might rush him as he reached the bottom and knock him over the edge. But even as I started to get up, I realized what they were doing.

51

They were chipping away at the footholds I had used in getting down. And they had only to knock off one or two and I was a prisoner right here, and could be left to starve to death. There would be no marks of violence on my body, and this was vastly preferable to a bullet wound that must be explained away.

"We aren't going to worry about you any more," Colin said after a while. "And if there are any tapes of yours that are a danger to us, we will have them."

My secretary, a trusting girl, would be alone. She would protect my property if she could—but against Floyd Reese or Jimbo Wells?

I could not wait. Somehow, some way, I had to get away from here.

Then above me I heard the grate of boots on rock, retreating footsteps . . . and then I was alone.

Chapter 6 ᗢᘐᘐᘐᘐᘐᘐᘐᘐᘐᘐᘐᘐᘐ

The sun was high, but it was cool within the walls of my prison. Above me was a narrow ribbon of blue, and straight before me the canyon, so narrow that in places one might almost have reached from side to side. Where I sat it was wider, but as it narrowed it took a slight bend, so that the curve of the wall closed off any glimpse of the outer world. That world, I knew, lay bright in the mid-day sun only a few hundred yards away.

For a long time I sat perfectly still. When one has lived in the wilderness one acquires a quality of stillness, and one learns to listen.

The sounds of the lonely places are subdued sounds. Once one becomes accustomed to those that prevail, such as the wind in the trees or in the grass, he soon begins to recognize those other, smaller sounds. He learns to know the sound of a bird rustling after food among the leaves, or the sounds made by small animals. He learns to distinguish between the sound of pebbles falling by some natural cause, and those disturbed by a step.

There is never complete silence. The wilderness is quiet, but there is always a faint, low rustle or murmur. Listening is an art to be cultivated; and the symphonies of the desert or the forest demand a finer ear than do the symphonies of the composers.

I knew that all that I possessed, all that I had tried to become, my very life, was at stake. This was no story I was writing, but reality itself, stark and terrible. Within the next few hours I must fight a battle to survive, a battle that would determine not only whether I would live or die, but also whether Belle would. And if we did die, an evil thing would remain in the world, destructive and unchecked.

Man has within himself the most powerful weapon ever developed—the human brain. If I were to survive now, it would be because what strength I possessed would be directed by the mind.

So I sat quietly, listening. The taint and turmoil of cities were gone from me. Minute by minute I had been reverting to the life of the mountains and the wilderness —back, if you will, to savagery. I was here in a savage land, and to survive I must be savage, even more so than they who hunted me.

Again my thoughts returned to the Alvarez brothers. They were part Apache, and undoubtedly their forebears were somewhere about when the Toomeys drove their cattle into the valley of the Verde. Little could have happened at that time without their knowledge.

I moved to the lip of the precipice and looked down. Even with rope and pitons descent would be next to impossible. And the way I had come was now even more impossible.

Upon the ledge where I stood there was a little sand trapped by the unevenness of the rock, and I examined this. There are few places in the mountains that are not visited by wild animals, and often their tracks can lead a man to water, to shelter, or even, as in such a case as mine, to escape.

But I was not to be so lucky. Nowhere on the ledge could I find any tracks, or any droppings that would indicate an animal had been here.

There was a little driftwood, which I gathered. It was enough, if used with care, for a small fire for one or perhaps two nights, and I knew these mountains well enough to know that when darkness came it would be cold. The place where I was caught was about a mile above sea level, and when the sun goes down it is not warm in that altitude, even in the middle of summer. I would build my fire near the rock, which would act as a reflector.

All this time there had been no shots. I had kept my thoughts away from Belle Dawson, who had gotten off at a dead run. She knew this country, and I told myself she must have found a hiding place. She had grown up here, and children often know the odd corners and hiding places better than adults do. There would be places where she had gone to be alone, places she had found when following animals, places she had come upon quite by chance. One of these places might be a hiding place for her. Yet even as I told myself this, I worried.

And then I thought of something else. Floyd Reese would not rest, simply knowing I was trapped. I had hurt him, hurt him physically and in his ego, and he would not be one to forgive. He had taken a beating from me, and he would want to inflict pain on me, to see me suffer, to gloat. He was that sort of man.

Floyd Reese would be coming here.

Shadows gathered in the canyon below, while gold rimmed the ridges above me. Carefully I put my fire together, and was about to sit down beside it when I had a new thought. It was impossible to go down, impossible to go back up, but what about going *out*?

I got up from the ground quickly. In three steps I was at the rim of the cliff and looking at the smooth walls that stretched away before me.

The idea of working along those cliffs that walled the

canyon on both sides had not occurred to me before. Now as I looked I could see nothing to give me hope— no crevice, no place where I could grasp a hold with hands or feet. Yet I would not accept the idea that I was finished. There had to be a way; if there was not, I would make one.

If I could find a way to work along the face of the rock, out from the ledge on which I stood, I might in time find some way either up or down.

Nobody needed to tell me how foolish it was to try such a thing alone. From time to time I had done a bit of rock climbing and knew the way of it, but here I had neither helpers nor equipment. I stood there until darkness came to the cleft in the rock, trying with every bit of my mind and memory to work out a way to do it.

It didn't matter that it was impossible—there was no other way. I might have tried to wait until a searching party came, but I knew my hunch about Reese was right. He would leave me here, all right, but with a bullet in me—not one to kill, just one to cripple or injure.

There would be a search party. I knew that, which Colin could not know. During the past ten years I had been too much in the public eye, I had too many friends. I knew they would come looking, and that Colin would have no choice but to let them come. They would scour the country with helicopters in the air and searching parties on the ground, and some of them, some of my old climbing friends, would be experts. They would know where to look.

And a lot of good it would do me, for if I stayed here I would be dead.

Under the overhang I struck a match, shielded it from the rising wind, and had a fire going. There was fuel enough, and more than enough, now that I proposed to make the attempt to escape. And after a while, with a gnarled old cedar root to hold the fire, I slept.

It was a cold, shivering dawn that awakened me—not quite dawn, but a paling sky. I drank water and teased the fire into a blaze. There was still a bright star hanging low in the sky. It would be gone in a moment, behind the cliffs along which I meant to climb.

There was no hopeful thought in me as I waited, for I knew that no man but a fool, or one in such a desperate plight as my own, would make such an attempt. There seemed not even a chance to begin it. A sheer face is never easy, even with ropes and pitons and help, and the way I must try was courting suicide. Suicide it would be, for I could not say I was ignorant of what I was attempting. And there was the uncomfortable realization that Reese might choose just that moment to return. With me out on the face of the cliff, and Reese with a rifle in his hands, he would have things just the way he wanted them, and it would be a pleasurable time for him.

I waited there, cursing myself for having been such a fool as to get into such a box. All the pleasures; everything good in life was behind me now. The books I wanted to write and had not written, the things I wanted to do . . . I'd bought myself a package of trouble because of a few fading sheets of paper found in the barrel of an old pistol.

Dawn found its way along the high cliffs, and a gnarled and dwarfed cedar held up its limbs in agonized gesture before the awakening light. Standing up, I put out the last of my fire—not that there was anything for it to reach out for, but the ways of habit are strong. The fire out, I stretched and stretched, loosening the muscles against the time for moving out, if there was a chance for that.

Here and there I seemed to see just a thread of passage along the rock face. On the right the rock bellied out, leaving an awkward hollow beneath it. My first move would be to get off the ledge itself and onto the face, and looking at it I felt the cold of fear begin to creep up my spine.

It was like glass—smooth and sheer. There might be an occasional meager hand hold, but I'd be swinging free and clear, hundreds of feet above the rocks below, and it was a prospect I had no taste for.

On the edge of the ledge I stood looking out, studying the cliff. Going down would be impossible. If I could make it at all from out there it would have to be up.

My eyes went to the left. There was the sheer drop to the rocks, but about six feet out was a cedar, a small tree with many stiff branches, some old, some young. Beyond the cedar, and several feet higher up, I could see what might be considered a narrow ledge. It was not even two inches wide, and looked to be about six feet long.

If I could get into that cedar and stand up, hoping it would not break, and then get my fingers on that ledge, I might inch along it, my body hanging against the rock . . . but where from that point?

I saw that there was a crack in the rock just beyond, a crack not over four or five inches wide at most . . . or so it appeared from where I stood. If I could reach that, I might use a lie-back—my feet against the far side of the crack, my hands pulling hard against the near side, and so holding myself up and climbing by opposing the one strength against the other, I might be able to climb.

But that twenty feet . . . I felt the cold sweat on my forehead and my hands were clammy. There would be no rope to hold me . . . a moment's weakness and I was finished. And always there would be the threat of Reese, who might suddenly arrive on the scene.

Above that twenty feet out there, was a ledge. It looked to be a foot wide, which was like a highway compared to what lay between where I stood and it. Beyond that ledge I could not see. I might get there and find myself helpless to go on—and once there I could not even die in comfort. It would be merely a matter of hanging on until I weakened and fell.

The cedar was craggy and old. Gray, jagged ends of ancient limbs thrust out through the green, and they could open a man wide if he fell against them. But there was no other way for it, and I had waited long enough.

I took off my coat and dropped it on the ledge, where

it could be seen if searchers came looking. Then, swinging my arms, I jumped.

For an instant I seemed to hang in the air, and then some of the cedar's branches were splintering under me, but the tree itself had kept its strength and it was sturdy. Some old limbs broke, but the tree held, and gingerly I eased my feet onto the thickest of the short branches.

Carefully I stood up, balancing myself. The tiny ledge was above me. Stretching my arms out, I was still a few inches short of reaching it. There was nothing else for it . . . a quick hop . . . my fingers caught, clung.

I swung against the face, then hung there still. Ever so gently, sweat streaming down my face, I worked my fingers along, my whole weight hanging from them.

Inch by inch, my mouth dry as dust, my breath coming hoarsely, I moved along the ledge. Once I thought I heard a sound . . . was Reese coming? Horror filled me. I did not want to die . . . I wanted, desperately, to live!

Halfway. Another inch . . . the strain on my fingers was almost intolerable.

The crack up which I must go was before me, and that meant an even greater strain. Suddenly my fingers encountered a small rock and some dust. For an instant I held myself still. If my fingers slipped on that dust . . . I moved them and the rock fell past my face, dust falling against my cheeks.

The crack opened beside me and I got a boot into it. My body was wet with sweat, as much from fear as from exertion.

One hand moved, turned, and the fingers hooked against the rock. Then I shifted my weight, getting the other foot against the far side of the rock. I dared not hold still; there was no place to rest, or even to catch a breath.

Using the lie-back, my weight hanging against my fingers while I pushed against the rock with my feet, I began to climb. Slowly . . . up . . . up . . . up.

All at once I knew I was going to make it. I was going to reach that ledge.

I grasped at the edge of it, and it crumbled under my fingers. Reaching out, I tested a further place, and got hold of it, then pulling against the rock I hauled myself up and got a knee on the ledge. Slowly, with infinite care, my palms reached up along the wall . . . up, up higher. Using the strength of one leg, I pulled up the other, then slowly stood up.

For a long moment I rested there, trembling like an aspen.

Behind me was the gulf of the canyon, before me sheer wall. Turning my head carefully, I looked along the ledge. It went out of sight under a bulging overhang where I must kneel down to pass.

Just then somewhere back of me I heard a rock roll, as if under a boot. Breathing hoarsely, I carefully worked along the ledge, eased myself to one knee, and edged under the overhang.

Behind me a voice called. "Sheridan?"

It was Reese, and he had not seen me yet. Under the bulge, where there was shadow, I remained immovable.

"Sheridan!" he called again. "That coat doesn't fool me. Not even a fly could go down that wall. I've stood at the base of it, and I know."

There was a long moment of stillness. I wanted to move—I wanted to get around the slight curve in the rock. But I dared not move, for to move was almost surely to be seen.

"Sheridan?" The voice was a little less sure now. "Come on, Sheridan. I've come to get you out of there." He was lying, for I could see the pistol in his hand, ready for a shot.

"It was all a mistake," he went on. "The boss wants to make it up to you. Come on out and I'll toss you a rope."

An inch . . . if I moved just an inch . . . I crawled my fingers forward along the ledge, held still, then lifted my knee ever so lightly and pushed it forward a little.

All was quiet behind me. I dearly wanted to look, but dared not.

He was walking around now; soon his eyes would go along the cliff. I did not think he could make me out, in the shadow as I was . . . but he might.

I eased my fingers along, and leaning my weight on my palm I hunched forward a little. Almost instantly there was a shot. A bullet struck the rock above me and ricocheted off down the canyon. Reese shouted some incomprehensible words at me, and fired again.

But the moment had given me time to move. The corner wasn't much, but I was around it, with a swell of the rock behind me.

But there was no time for elation. Glancing quickly around, I saw the ledge on which I stood ran only a few feet farther, but beyond it was a chimney, a cleft in the rock that appeared to be several feet deep, and from three feet wide opposite where I stood, to five or six feet wide at the bottom, a good hundred and fifty feet down.

Above, the chimney narrowed to slightly less than three feet, and led to the top of the mesa, where it widened out into a saucer-like depression. However, I dared not try to climb to the top, for Reese would be riding along there soon, and there would be no escape for me on the top. My only chance was to descend the chimney, get on down the slope, and try to find a horse or some other means of escape, or perhaps get to a telephone.

It did not take me long to reach the chimney. A risky step and a swing into the narrow space in the rock, my knees against one side, my back and hands against the other, using the opposition of forces to work my way down the narrow cleft.

I thought of Belle, who must be somewhere down there. Without a horse there was no chance of finding her in this rough country. Yet my mind would not dismiss the thought of her, worrying over what Colin Wells might do now that he felt assured of my imminent death; for it would be hours before he could learn that I had, at least for the time, escaped.

It was growing warm. The sky above was a pleasant blue, with a jet trail marking a streak of passage across it.

High overhead, winging slowly above the desert, a buzzard hung in mid-air.

When I reached the last few feet I just let go and dropped, landing on the slope with bent knees, and moving forward even as I touched the ground

My thoughts ran swiftly ahead. There was a walkie-talkie back in the jeep, but that was some miles away, and Reese would not be likely to call for help until he was sure he had lost me. Then he might get in touch with the other hands by some means, and they would be hunting me as soon as they learned about it.

What I needed now was a weapon, and I needed it desperately.

It was almost unbelievable that a great city lay not many miles away, for here all was wilderness, unchanged since the days when John and Clyde Toomey had first arrived.

And then, suddenly, I knew where I was going.

Chapter 7

I was going to Lost River.

It could not be far from here, and the description of its location had been graphic enough. It must be a location similar to that of Fossil Springs, somewhat to the north, where a power station had been developed.

Lost River was literally that: a river in a small rocky basin, that emerged from the ground, bursting forth in great volume, ran along for a short distance through a rocky channel, and then disappeared underground. The water, John Toomey had said, was clear and cold, and not mineralized to any extent. By the time I reached the place I would be in desperate need of a drink, unless I came upon water from some other source.

It was not likely that I would ever get this close to

the place again, so I wanted now to verify what Toomey had said about it. If I could do that, and by some means gain entry to the old stone fort on the ranch, I would have my story.

But now it was no longer merely a story I wanted. At first I had been unwilling to believe what was happening to me, and then had been desperately occupied with making an escape; now I was getting thoroughly mad. Anger was stirring deep within me. There had been flashes of dislike, irritation, and fear, but the anger that came to me now was no sudden emotion that would pass off. It was a deep, abiding anger, with a desire to strike back hard.

Nothing in life had ever taught me to fight merely to win. This had to be more than victory.

I was, I told myself, an easy-going man. The old knockabout days were gone, the war a thing of the past. Violence had been put behind me. I was a civilized human being.

But now I had been set upon. I had been attacked and had been forced to run, and how I hated the thought! I had been forced to hide. I had been taunted and shot at. Above all—and this offended my ego—I had been taken lightly.

But now I had a deeper purpose. The mere story was no longer the important thing. Now I wanted to uncover what they were trying so desperately to hide, and to destroy them with it.

In the back of my mind, however, there was something else. There were two men named Toomey who had driven their cattle west, only to be, if my guess was right, murdered and robbed. Somehow in reading and re-reading those few pages of the journal, in delving into their former lives in Texas, I had found a real affection for those two strong, independent men who carried on in the best American tradition. Yes, I will admit it: Along with my anger, there was a definite desire to avenge them, to prove they had not failed.

Pausing now in the shadow of the rock, I studied the terrain below and before me. From now on, every step must be guarded, every movement cautious. If they were waiting for me down there, I must not let them find me, nor must I come upon some of them by sheer accident.

Carefully, then, I moved out. Holding to the shadows that remained, moving off down the slope on a wide angle, I used the frequent clumps of cedar, the scattered rocks, the desert brush for cover.

Down below me I saw that there was an ancient Indian trail along the bottom.

It was very still. Already heat gathered in the depths of the canyons. Warily, I moved along, seeing no tracks of horse or man. Once I saw those of a deer or a bighorn sheep, but in the soft sand there was no exact identification. Here and there, snagged among the boulders, there were tangled heaps of driftwood, and I watched for something I might use as a weapon that would be equally useful as a walking staff.

Sweat was beading my forehead and began to trickle down my neck. From time to time, I paused and listened. Now I was a hunted man, hunted by those who would undoubtedly kill me on sight, and without a gun I was helpless, or nearly so.

Again and again I found myself stopping, expecting some sound, expecting eyes to be looking at me from somewhere not far away. I knew that the desert mountains can do this to a man, even to a man not in my desperate situation, and often before when in no danger I had felt the same way.

Southwest of me rose the bulk of New River Mesa. Once, long ago, I had camped in a canyon under its cliffs. It was country I thought I would remember, and if I could get a good drink at Lost River, I might strike due south and climb the mesa. There had been an old outlaw hide-out on the north side of the canyon.

Suddenly, without any warning, there was a rattle of hoofs, and I heard a man swear angrily.

Instantly I dropped behind some coarse brush and rocks. It was no proper hiding place, but there was nothing else. As I went down on one knee, my hand closed around a smooth, water-worn rock about as large as my fist.

The rider emerged from a narrow branch canyon just ahead of me, a canyon that until that moment I had not realized was there. He drew up and looked around.

He was still muttering to his horse, which evidently had slipped on the rock. After that one glance around, he dug into his shirt pocket for the makings and began to build a cigarette. He was half turned away from me, but I knew the danger of being seen from the corner of the eye, almost greater than being seen when directly in front, and waited.

He was not over twenty yards off, but too far for me to throw a rock with accuracy even if I had been sure of my aim, which I wasn't. It had been years since I'd thrown any kind of a ball, and at baseball I'd been no great shakes. But I dearly wanted that horse; and if not the horse, at least a gun.

Thoughtfully, trying not to look directly at him for fear something in my concentration would attract him, I studied the terrain between us. It was ground that would be easier to cross quietly than some I had crossed in Korea under equally bad conditions—but I was several years away from Korea.

If he turned in any direction he was almost sure to see me. With infinite care I moved a foot to my right, then moved my body and my other foot. Now I was directly behind him. I stood up, as intent on the horse as on the man, for the horse's range of vision was greater, and of the two I feared he would be most alert.

Judging the sand, I took a long step toward them, and then another. The wind was away from the horse and toward me, so I tried one more step, and still another. Now a large rounded boulder was in the way. Crouching, I went around it to the right, and stepped down to a flat rock.

Two more steps I managed, and then the horse side-stepped quickly and snorted. Instantly, I ran toward them.

The rider saw me then, and dropped his hand for his gun.

The days of the fast draw were past, and his was no better than average. His horse was moving nervously, and I was coming at him, but as his fingers closed about the gun butt I let fly with my rock, throwing it with a bowling motion, and off my fingertips. I was hoping for nothing more than to make him duck and so give me time to close in, but even though he jerked his head back, the rock caught him on the point of the chin.

His gun was coming free of the holster, but it went off as his finger tightened convulsively. The sudden shot burned a streak along the flank of the horse and the animal leaped. That, coupled with my thrown rock, knocked him from the saddle. Rushing in, I swung a long right as he hit the ground and caught him flush on the jaw. Something crunched under my fist, and he screamed in agony. His jaw, had been broken by the rock, and the blow from my fist had shattered it.

His half-drawn gun had dropped back into the holster, and I jerked it from him. While he held his jaw and moaned, I stripped off his gun belt.

Then, ignoring him, I looked around for the horse. The frightened animal had run off a hundred yards or so, stepped on the trailing reins, and stopped. I wanted the horse, but I wanted the rifle in the scabbard on the saddle even more.

Leaving the cowhand clutching his jaw and making moaning sounds, I walked toward the horse. He let me come close, then trotted off a few steps. I walked after him, talking softly, and finally he let me come close enough to take the reins. A moment later and I was in the saddle.

That shot would bring trouble pretty soon, and I had no idea of being there when it arrived. The difficulty was that there were few possible routes of travel at the bottom of the canyons.

Avoiding the New River trail, I went over a saddle in the hills to a trail that skirted Grapevine Canyon. Then cutting back to Gray's Gulch, I skirted the towering mass of New River Mesa, and saw tracks in the trail ahead of me.

A walking horse. I recognized the tracks even before I heard her speak.

"Was that you who shot?"

It was Belle. She was sitting the saddle in the deep shadow beside a dense mass of juniper.

"I was shot at. Or rather, he was drawing for a shot when I got to him."

"You *killed* him?"

"No . . . but he's dismounted now, and he has a broken jaw. He's out of it—you can be sure of that."

"Where were you going?" she asked.

I shrugged. "Robbers' Roost, or some place around there. What we'd better do is get clear out of this part of the country."

"And leave my ranch?"

"You've left it before. Go back with a deputy U.S. Marshal. That's what I'd do."

We walked our horses down the draw. The mesa cast a shadow over most of the trail, allowing it to emerge into the light only at rare intervals. Suddenly, I realized that I was hungry.

There were saddlebags on the horse, but there was nothing to eat in them. There was tobacco, but I was not a smoker. Other than that, I found only matches, some odds and ends of rawhide, a handful of cartridges for the .303 rifle, and two more cartridges for the pistol.

"If we get out alive," Belle said.

I looked at her. I'd been thinking the same thing, but did not know how much she realized the situation. Of course, they knew where we were, within a few miles. By now they might have found the man I'd hurt; or they would find him before dark. I hoped for his sake they would find him, for he was out of it as far as I was concerned, and badly injured.

Cities and highways and people were not many miles away from us, no distance at all as such things are figured

66

in these days, but between ourselves and whatever refuge they offered, those miles were all desert and mountains. And men close by were searching for us by horse and jeep.

"What is worrying me right now," I said, my eyes searching the hills, "is Pio Alvarez."

"Pio?"

So, as we rode deeper and deeper into the canyon, I told her what I knew about Pio. I told her about Korea and that cold and bitter retreat, and how Pio and I had fought side by side, had cowered together among the rocks and brush, had crept for miles across country. There was a lot I did not tell, for those who have not experienced such things cannot understand. To sheltered and peaceful people who live in warm homes and sit in comfortable chairs and sleep safely at night, there can be no realization of the desperation of men running and fighting for their lives against enormous odds.

We had killed, Pio and I, killed with skill and ruthlessness and with shocking effect. Those who came between us and freedom had little chance against us; they were killed and left there on the ground.

I knew Pio, or I thought I did; and Pio's brothers had been killed. He would know why, and by whom. "They haven't any idea what they've started," I told Belle. "Pio is one of the greatest guerilla fighters I have ever seen . . . and there isn't an ounce of mercy in him."

We found the stone-walled cave where Lost River ran— cold, clear water rising from the depths of the earth, running a few yards on the surface, and then disappearing into the rock again. We found the river in a niche in the rocks where few would think to look. There was a hollow there with trees and brush, and only one opening that anyone was likely to find.

But there was another opening, and the journal of John Toomey had told me where to look for it.

"We haven't any food," Belle said. "All they have to do is hold us here and wait for us to starve."

"Maybe," I responded.

67

Rock walls rose on either side of us, and entry to the cave where the river emerged was through a narrow cleft in the rock. At times in the bygone ages the river must have swelled to flood dimensions, for the walls of the niche into which we had come were water-worn. They were under-cut, offering some shelter.

It was very still here. There was only the sound of the water rustling by, running swiftly over polished rocks, with only a few pebbles at the bottom. It ran along until almost outside the cave, then suddenly dipped into the rock and vanished with a hollow sound, falling into an unknown vastness. Inside the niche the space measured only a few square yards.

"You knew about this place?" Belle asked.

Listening, I did not answer at once. Then I said, "Did you ever hear of John or Clyde Toomey?"

"Toomey? No, I don't think so." But she hesitated, her eyes searching mine. "Why do you ask?"

"Because I've a fool idea that they were behind all this. I say a fool idea, because both men have been dead for ninety years."

I changed the subject. "How did your family happen to settle here?"

"Just as every pioneer family did, I suppose. They came west, found a likely spot, and built a home."

"They built it?"

"Not really. I did hear once that it was built by another man, somebody who worked for my grandfather or great grandfather. They never told me much about the place, but they were adamant that it should never be sold. That's why when the will was made, the place was left in such a way that the property would remain in the family, no matter what."

"What was your great grandfather's name?"

"Dawson, I suppose. I was never very interested in such things, and nobody ever talked about him. In fact, Dad and Mother always insisted that the matter never be mentioned. But I overheard some talk between them and asked questions."

"That man who worked for your great grandfather? Do you remember his name?"

"Oh, yes. It was Bal Moore. He filed on this land, and he deeded it to his boss. They did that back in cattle days."

It had been a means to holding more land, which ranchers had used in all parts of the range country. Their hands would file on claims, usually on sites where there was water, and then either sell out to their boss, or arrange some deal by which the land would fall to the boss, giving him control over the water. Hence, control over the range.

"What happened to Bal?"

"He was killed. I believe it was by Apaches."

The pieces were beginning to fall into place. Bal Moore's name was familiar. He had been *segundo* on the drive west, and was mentioned twice in the journal's pages that I had. He had been tough, and reliable, and he knew cattle. Above all, he had worked for the Toomeys since before the war.

We were not safe here. That was the thought in the back of my mind as we talked, and one part of my consciousness was drifting, searching for a way out. The mountains, of course, are filled with odd corners where a man can hide; the trouble was that such a man as Reese would know them all. Colin, too, would probably be familiar with them. The Roost, I knew, was not far away—just across the mesa, in fact—but the chances were they knew of that, too.

By now they would have moved to guard every route out of the ranch area; once we got outside and could talk, they knew there would be trouble. But though we dared not remain where we were, I had no idea of where to go.

At the moment it was comfortable to wait, for no man can run without considering where he is going. We needed this respite, and despite the fact that we seemed to be in a trap here, there was a way out if John Toomey was right. For he had tried a way out from here, where he had seemed to be caught. It was in this place that he scratched the last words of his journal, on the margins of the pages torn from the book.

Believing the journal might be destroyed, John Toomey had tried to leave a record of truth behind him, hoping the broken and discarded pistol would not be examined . . . and it was not.

Restlessly, I got to my feet. I knew we had little time. With the rifle I could stand them off for a while, but no doubt they would know about how much ammunition I had, and when it was gone they could move in for the kill—or they would simply let us remain here and starve. I had escaped from one trap only to get into another . . . unless the escape route mentioned by John Toomey would work for me.

He had written of the route he intended to take, but John Toomey had never escaped alive from the same trap in which we found ourselves.

"Dan," Belle said, "are we going to get out? Or are they going to kill us here?"

"I don't know, Belle," I had to answer. "I really don't know."

Chapter 8 ~~~~~~~~~~~~~~~~~~~~~~~~~

The hollow in which we now stood had been created by falling water. From somewhere above, long ago, a stream had tumbled over the cliff's edge, gradually hollowing out this basin, then spilling out through the crack by which we had entered, and so into the valley below.

This much was obvious from the appearance of the rock and the basin itself, and this much John Toomey, wounded and trapped, had figured out for himself. But he had gone further, deducing that the hollowing action had been accomplished by Lost River itself. The stream that once had fallen over the edge above had found another way, creeping into some crack and widening it until the entire flow could plunge into the cave and emerge below.

John Toomey's last words, scratched on the margins of the pages of his journal before he concealed them in the barrel of the Bisley Colt, had said as much. He added that he was now going into the cave from which the water emerged, and try to climb out.

Had he succeeded in that climb? Probably not, but if he had, he must have been found and killed shortly after, for he had never returned to pick up the broken pistol.

He had tried. Wounded and desperate, he had tried. He had dared to crawl into that black opening filled with the roar of rushing water.

Somehow, just the thought of that wounded man, hounded to this place by men who planned his murder, having the courage to crawl into that black hole gave me confidence.

I spoke again. "We'll get out, Belle," I said. "We'll make it."

The guns gave me confidence, for I had qualified as Expert with six weapons during the training before Korea, and I'd had more than my share of fighting in Korea and Vietnam. If they wanted my scalp they were going to have to buy it the hard way.

How long until dark? I looked longingly at the sky. We had a chance of riding out under cover of darkness, and might even make it through. If we could make it to the village of Cave Creek or to the highway, we'd have a chance. But I knew they would have all the trails covered by men ready and willing to shoot.

We might go over the mountains. If we could get across to the Agua Fria, the country around Mayer and Dewey was familiar to me. And if we could get to a telephone I could call Tom Riley.

Shadows were gathering in the draws and canyons, and there was a faint coolness in the air. Rifle in hand, I went to the opening and looked out. Belle sat quietly. There were no sounds but the pleasant murmur of the water and the crunching of the horses' teeth and as they grazed on the coarse grass. These were pleasant in the stillness.

Then, some distance off, I heard a plane. Belle heard it, too. She got up and came to me quickly.

"Dan, that's Colin. He has his own plane, you know."

"Why the plane?" I asked. "He must know where we are . . . or just about where."

"I've seen them hunt coyotes from the plane," she answered.

Of course. I had often seen coyotes hunted from the air, and a man could shoot from a plane. But this was rough country for that, unlike the Texas, Oklahoma, or Kansas country that was relatively wide open and flat where they hunted from planes.

I spoke quietly to Belle. "If you get out of here, go to Tom Riley. He's investigating the Alvarez killing and he strikes me as a solid citizen. Get to him and tell him everything you know."

"What's it all about, Dan?"

"I think you know just as much as I do. Two men named Toomey drove a herd of cattle out here in 1872. They dropped from sight and the cattle disappeared. I think the men were murdered and the cattle stolen.

"I have reason to believe they had legal claim to a large area in this region, and that the murderers took over their claims and have lived on them ever since. They have never offered any land for sale, and I don't believe there has ever been a serious title search made. Any heirs of the Toomeys that there may have been did not even know they were heirs, or that there was anything to inherit. Or if they did know, they were afraid to make any claim for fear of what might happen.

"I believe that since that time the Wells family has lived in fear of losing the place, and that their fear has grown in direct ratio to the value of the land. I also believe that you may be one of the Toomey heirs . . . but all I have to base it on is a hunch."

By now the crack through which we had entered was in

darkness, and a vague twilight lay upon the land outside, a twilight in which nothing moved.

"All right," I said. "Mount up."

Belle swung easily into the saddle and gathered her reins.

There was nothing for it but to ride. To stay bottled up here would gain us nothing; and while they might be waiting somewhere outside, waiting to get us in the open, the light was already bad for shooting, and soon it would be gone entirely. We had our slim chance now, and I meant for us to take it.

So we rode out into the open . . . and nothing happened. Somewhere a quail called, but I was sure it was a real quail. We walked our horses along the slope, moving from one clump of cedars to the next. The light was almost gone when Belle's horse snorted and a figure lunged up from the ground and seized the bridle. Another grabbed my horse's and Reese's voice came from the shadows. "Drop that rifle, Sheridan!"

A man rode up beside me and reached for the rifle and I swung it—a short, brutal smash against his skull with the butt, as against a ripe melon. Then I rolled from the saddle, hit the dirt behind one of the thick cedars, and remained motionless for a moment.

Horses were rearing and plunging, and I ran, crouching, to the next cedar, slid a few feet on a steep slope, and swung into deeper shadow among a clump of cedar a good sixty feet away.

Reese was swearing as he lunged into the group. "Where is he? Damn it, what have I got here, a bunch of tinhorns? *Where is that man?*"

Had I hesitated even an instant when I left the saddle they would never have given me the chance to escape. It was the immediate move that caught them off-guard. And I was still armed.

Belle had sat perfectly still, simply waiting. "You'd better take care of that man on the ground," she said calmly. "I am afraid he's badly hurt."

73

Reese paid no attention to her words. "Wait until I get my hands on him." His voice was hoarse with anger.

"You tried that once," Belle said, "and you got the worst of it."

There was the thud of a blow, followed by a moment of silence, then Belle said, "You're practically safe, striking a woman with her hands tied, Floyd. I always thought you were a coward. I wonder if you could really whip a woman, on equal terms?"

He struck her again, and I came off the ground, hot with fury.

"Cut it out, Floyd!" It was one of the riders who spoke. "Let's find Sheridan. I didn't hire out to fight women."

"By God!" Reese's voice shook with rage. "I'll—"

"You think before you do, Floyd." The rider's voice was calm. "You ain't goin' to get no place fightin' with your own men. You've got yourself a packet of trouble right now."

Easing back a few steps, I made a miscalculation and a rock gave away behind me. I fell three feet to the bottom of a ditch cut by run-off water, amid a rattle of stones.

Instantly there was rush of hoofs. "Get him!" somebody shouted, and at least three riders came at me.

My rifle came up, caught one of them in the sights, and I let go my shot. Then I dropped down into the ditch and scrambled on over sharp stones and gravel.

Bullets *whapped* against rocks or whipped by above me, but I was moving swiftly, and under good cover. I had no idea whether I'd hit the man I shot at, but from now on they were going to be a lot more careful hunting around in the dark. No man wants to die, and it was going to be obvious that somebody might . . . not necessarily me.

The chase suddenly stopped. "Listen!" Reese shouted. "He can't get far!"

For the moment I was in soft sand, and by now it was completely dark, so I kept moving. There was small chance they would risk killing Belle while I was free, but

74

there was nothing I could do about it for the moment.

When I paused at last I was well up on the side of the mesa and several hundred feet above the trail. At this point the mesa was easily scaled. At places it might even have been done by a man on horseback, or so it had seemed by day, though no trail led upward that I had seen. Certainly it could be scaled by a man on foot.

But no longer was I thinking of my own escape. All I could think of was Belle in the hands of the Wells outfit. Somehow she must be freed from them.

Whatever sense those men out there had possessed was lost to them now. It must have seemed fairly simple to them to invite me to the ranch where an "accident" would occur. But their plans had failed, and they were growing increasingly desperate and reckless.

In my dealings with criminals in the past one thing had become obvious, that all were incurable optimists, as well as egotists. They were confident their plans would succeed, and had nothing but contempt for the law and for the law-abiding citizen.

Colin Wells could have no appreciation of the patience and thoroughness of a good police officer such as Tom Riley. Riley had connected Manuel Alvarez with me. By now, if not before, he would have a question in his mind about the death of Pete Alvarez on the Wells ranch. His patient checking or that of his department would undoubtedly turn up the fact (printed occasionally on the jacket of my books) that I had served in Korea. And undoubtedly Pio's military record was included in the facts in the hands of the police.

In these days there are few areas in the life of a man that remain secret from even the most casual investigation, and Riley would not be casual. Without a doubt Colin Wells already represented a large question in the mind of Tom Riley, but this Wells would have no reason to suspect.

Although several of the ranch force were deputies, it was unlikely they had participated in any police work other than that connected with their own neighboring properties, or with criminal activity in the immediate area.

But Colin Wells knew that our escape from the ranch would certainly mean an investigation. He would have all the witnesses, but even if he made it impossible to prove a case against him, the clouded title of the ranch would be exposed and an investigation begun to establish ownership.

Suddenly, I knew what I must do. I must get back to the ranch and use the telephone there. I must get an emergency call through to Tom Riley in the city. He could start the wheels of the law rolling even out here.

We were twenty miles or more from the Wells ranch house. Going over rough country and avoiding trails most of the time, it would take me a good many hours to reach it.

I thought of the Bar-Bell, Benton Seward's place. It was less than half the distance, but Seward would be home and so would his hands. In between was Belle's place on Cougar Canyon, but I doubted if there was a telephone there. I could not recall that she had said anything about one.

Well, if I was lucky and didn't fall off a cliff in the darkness, I could perhaps make Seward's place before daybreak. With a horse I might have made it in less than two hours, but I knew rough country too well to underestimate the time required to cross it.

Ignoring the sounds from behind me, I started out at a fast pace. I came down off the mesa and crossed Cave Creek, hit the old trail that skirted Cramm Mountain, and broke into a trot. Trotting fifty steps and walking fifty, I paused occasionally to listen, and I took time to glance at my watch. Presently I was climbing the old Indian trail, scarcely visible as a faint gray line, that led across Bulldog Mesa.

The trail was an unexpected break. My eyes, long accustomed to looking for such trails, had picked it out of the gloom. When one has ridden such trails for miles across country, one acquires almost an instinct for them.

Often I had found and followed trails that were invisible to anyone else not equally experienced.

When I reached Benton Seward's and crouched beside the stable, my wrist-watch told me it was just past three o'clock in the morning. It was very dark, and there was no sound. My eyes, accustomed to the darkness, picked out objects easily. The large ranch house, built of native stone, faced west toward the mountains. On the far side, away from where I now waited, I knew there was a picture window that looked across the Verde. On that side there was a terrace.

Seward was undoubtedly here, and some of the ranch hands would be sure to be around. There should be a dog, but so far there had been no barking. The last thing I wanted was to be set upon by a dog just as I was about to enter the house.

Circling behind the stable, I worked around to the far side. Moving on cat feet, I slipped over the low wall at the edge of the terrace and crossed to the house. The sliding glass door moved easily under my hand—locks were not much used in ranch country—and I stepped through it. Once in the room, I stood still, listening.

The rifle I had left by the door, but the pistol was tucked in my waistband, ready for use. The room was dark, but I could make out a TV set very dimly, and a sofa and a table. My own form blacked out by the shadow of the curtains, I waited and studied the room as best I could. There were two doors, and what seemed to be a bar, and there should be a telephone.

There did not seem to be one on the bar . . . nor on the table. With the greatest care, I left my place and moved into the room, edging toward one of the doors. The sofa was so dimly seen that I could not be sure whether someone might be lying on it . . . there was not.

At the door I paused and listened, but I heard no sound. I put out a hand to the knob, and gently I turned it. Slowly, I eased the door open.

My heart was pounding, my mouth felt dry. I left the

door slightly ajar, since there was no breeze stirring, and stepped into the space beyond. On my right was a door opening into a kitchen, and there on the table, just inside the door, was a telephone. Carefully, I eased the phone from the cradle and dialed Operator. When she answered I started to speak.

"This is the Bar-Bell ranch. There has been a murder and an attempted murder on the Colin Wells ranch. Please report this to Tom Riley of the—"

"Put it down."

The voice was cold and level, and filled with menace. Doris Wells, in an enticing green negligee, held an altogether unenticing black pistol. She held it very steadily, right at my belt buckle.

"Put it down—carefully."

As I started to lower it to the cradle she stepped around me and deftly took it in her left hand. "Operator," she said, "we're having a party. I am afraid some of our guests have become somewhat intoxicated. This is their idea of a joke. I'm sorry."

Even as she was speaking, I moved, reaching for the gun. She tried to step back, tripped over a chair, and the gun went off . . . and then I grabbed her wrist and twisted the gun free.

Quickly, I flattened myself against the wall, holding the gun ready. She got up off the floor, gathering her negligee together. "You fool!" she exclaimed. "What do you hope to gain by that?"

She gestured . . . the telephone had dropped back on the cradle. Had the circuit closed before the gun went off? My good sense told me the report must have been too late to have been heard; or if it had been, the operator might not realize it had been a shot . . . a champagne cork would make a not dissimilar sound.

"What you do not seem to realize," I said, "is that this has already gotten out of hand. Whatever you hoped to accomplish by inviting me here has already failed."

"You're still here. We've had a lot of experience with

cow thieves, you know. Not one of them ever got off our property."

"*Your* property?"

The skin around her eyes tightened. "*Our* property!" she repeated.

"You don't seem to realize that killing me wouldn't help in the least. Whether you know it or not, I have a certain following, a lot of people like to read my books. My death would have my publisher searching for every scrap I had written, and putting it in the hands of some good writer for completion, if that was necessary. So the very book you're trying to stop would be published anyway.

"After some litigation you would lose the ranch, but you would still be free. What you are asking for now is a death penalty."

"Don't be silly." Her tone was contemptuous. "Nothing has changed, nothing will change."

"This much has changed." The voice came from behind my shoulder, for I'd half turned from the wall, and it was Benton Seward's voice. "Drop the gun, Sheridan."

Without shifting position, I glanced around at him. He held a shotgun, and it was aimed at me. I smiled at him and said, "Seward, you've seen too many movies. In the movies they always drop their guns, don't they? That's because the people who write the script were never really in a spot like this. I am not going to drop this gun, and even if you shoot me I'll kill Doris. I'll shoot at least three times, Seward. Two of them for Doris, one for you."

"Drop it!" Seward said sharply, but somehow there was less assurance in his voice.

"Want to get shot in the face, Doris? He's banking on that shotgun, and it's as dangerous to you as to me. I don't know how much training he's had at this, but I had a lot of it in Korea and Vietnam. I may get it, but I'll take both of you with me."

Once I'd lost that gun and the one in my waistband, I

would have lost any chance I had for survival. No matter what Seward might do—and he struck me as wanting the profit without the risk—Doris wouldn't hesitate to shoot. I was banking on Seward chickening out . . . I didn't think he had it in him to risk a shoot-out.

"Anyway," I added, "I've called the law. You'll have them all over the place, asking everybody questions . . . all sorts of questions."

"The call didn't get through," Doris said. She began edging around the table to try to get closer to Seward, but I motioned her back. Suddenly, there was a roar of a motor close by, and I realized I had been hearing it for several minutes; now a car came charging into the yard.

"It's the police," I said, but I didn't believe it.

Seward lowered the shotgun and turned his head toward the window. That was all I needed. As his head turned and the shotgun muzzle lowered, I was moving. On my second step my shoulder hit him and knocked him off balance back to the wall. He lost his grip on the shotgun and it fell, and I went out of the door where I'd come in, catching up the rifle as I left.

I was on the opposite side of the house from the arriving car. The corral was out there, bathed in light. Somebody inside the house was yelling, and suddenly the car roared into action, backed up, throwing light past the corner of the house. I heard it lunge forward and sweep around, and I knew that in a moment I would be caught in the full glare of the headlights.

Dropping to a knee close to the terrace wall, I emptied Doris' pistol into the glare of light. The glass of the headlight tinkled, and beyond the light someone screamed.

Then the light had me and I was running. But I ran toward them, not away, feeling that the quickest way into the concealment of darkness was behind the car.

As I ran I fired the rifle, levered a bullet into the chamber, and fired again. Then I was past the jeep. Somebody grabbed at me and I caught him in the face with a butt-stroke from the rifle, and then I ran on, straight into the darkness.

Behind me I heard the jeep smash into the wall, heard the tires scream on gravel as it turned; but the place was tight and the jeep had to be backed and turned again before the light could be thrown toward me. They were one moment too late, for by that time I was in the brush beyond the corral.

There I lay still, gasping for breath and listening to the confusion at the house. A babble of voices, someone swearing, and the strident, angry voice of Doris. She was shouting hoarsely, but under the sound of her voice I could hear Benton Seward, protesting . . . arguing.

Just then there was a rifle shot. It was fired from high up, behind me and on my left, from somewhere up on the ridge. The bullet smashed into the jeep.

A scream sounded and I could hear them all running for cover. Doris shouted, *"That's not him! That's not him, I tell you! It couldn't be!"*

A second shot came, and then a third . . . Suddenly the jeep exploded in a burst of flame, and the flame ran along the ground, following the line of spilled gasoline.

Lying still, I waited. That must be Pio, somewhere up in the rocks. Pio would be wanting to immobilize them, to tie them down.

Waiting no longer, I turned, and ducking from bush to bush, I started up the steep ridge. I wanted to find Belle, to reach her and get out of here together, away from the Wells ranch and all it meant.

I crouched for a moment on the hillside and watched the burning jeep. The dark figures around it had disappeared. Floyd Reese hadn't been down there, nor Colin. Mark Wilson had been—Mark Wilson, the stocky, powerfully built man who had followed me in the city. . . . How long ago had that been?

Then I went on climbing the slope in the darkness, and for the first time I realized how tired I was. Whatever else happened, I must find some place and sleep. . . . And I'd had nothing to eat—somehow, somewhere, I must get food.

Suddenly I remembered the sign left beside the trail.

Hadn't that sign indicated that there would be a camp? And hadn't it meant that I was to come when I could? It surely could not be far, perhaps no more than two or three miles away.

There was no way of knowing whether the operator had believed me or Doris . . . Doris might be known to her, for operators usually knew the people on rural lines; if so, it would be Doris she would believe. If she heard the shot she might report it to the authorities, but there was no certainty of that.

In the meantime, I needed rest and food, and needed to find Belle. Rest and food I might find wherever Pio was.

His leaving the sign for me was typical of him. It was at once a reminder of the old days, and of the old way of designating a company or battalion area. He probably discounted the chance of Colin or Reese knowing what it indicated, but more than likely he didn't care. If I knew Pio, he would be holed up in some place that could only be approached across an open area that offered a good field of fire . . . or one that offered opportunity for ambush.

When I reached the summit of the ridge I was all in, and sat down. It was cold, and a wind was blowing. Far below I could see the lights of the ranch house. Off to the north I could see specks of light that must be the Wells ranch.

It was almost daybreak, and far away in the east beyond the Tonto country the sky was growing lighter. Finding a crevice in the rocks on the summit, I crawled in, and huddled there out of the wind, I slept.

When I woke it was broad daylight. A glance at my watch . . . it was just past seven.

For a minute or two I lay still and listened. At first there was no sound but the wind. Then I sensed a vague whispering, rustling sound. I lifted my head cautiously.

A covey of blue quail were not ten feet away from me. I held still, and they moved off slowly. If aware of my presence, they were not disturbed by it.

Easing out of the crack in the rock, I lay on my

stomach, looking down at the ranch. In the yard were the charred remains of the jeep, but there was no person in sight. After a few minutes a man came out of the bunkhouse, stretched, and walked away toward the corral. He stopped once, studying the ground . . . looking at tracks, no doubt.

After giving careful study to the slope of the mountain to see if anyone moved there, I turned around and looked over my present position. The mountain that fell away so steeply on the side overlooking the ranch, on the other side fell gradually into a valley where cattle grazed. At the bottom I could see a trail . . . evidently the one from Belle Dawson's ranch to the Wells place.

Pio Alvarez had been on this summit last night, of that I felt sure. That he was still here was doubtful; knowing Pio, I knew he would never trust himself to only one hide-out. He would have several, and would move around from one to the other, probably never sleeping in the same place two nights in succession.

Moving back from the crest, I stood up and started down the other side of the mountain, angling northwest toward the place where Pio had left his sign.

Soon I was among the trees, for the top of Cedar Mountain was well covered, the cedars giving way here and there to tall pines. In places the trees were scattered, in others they were quite thick. Deer trails were here, and because of the carpet of needles, it was easier walking. I moved warily. Several times I saw tracks, apparently fresh.

"Hiya, keed!"

The greeting stopped me in my tracks. Though I was glad to hear that voice, I was not too pleased at being taken unawares.

Pio Alvarez had always been more Apache than Mexican, and he showed it now in the ease with which he came down through the trees. He was a stocky, powerful man with a tough, reckless grin. I had always been a little wary of him in the old days, for as close as we had been, I knew him for a dangerous man with volatile, uncertain moods. How he felt toward me I had never really known, but there was one thing I did know: With any lesser man I'd never have made it back to our lines in Korea.

"You have troubles, hey?" He squatted on his heels and dug out the makings, offering them to me.

"I don't smoke."

"Ah? This I remember. I don't have to share tobac' with you." He looked up at me out of flat black eyes. "You get away now, hey? You go?"

"They've got Belle Dawson. They'll kill her, Pio."

"Sure." He shrugged. "They have to keel her. The rancho belong to her." Then he added, "They keel her sister."

"They said it was an accident."

He grinned wickedly. "Plenty accident happen. Plenty. She keel him, too."

"She did?"

"Sure. I see it. Two, three days they scout around to decide where the car go—Aukie, Colin, an' Jimbo. I see them—I watch. One day Aukie comes in the car with her. I see door on his side swing open. He say somet'ing to her, start to jump. She grab him and hang on. She good one. Plenty good. She die, he die."

"You saw it?"

"Si."

"You didn't report it?"

He looked at me as if I were a fool. "The Law look for me. Colin Wells is after me for rustle steers. I report *him?*"

He smoked in silence. He had a Winchester, and he wore a belt gun. His hat was old and battered and he had on a scratched and cracked leather jacket, with worn levis.

"I've got to get Belle Dawson away. I'll let the Law do the rest."

"They are the Law," Pio said contemptuously. "They make the law."

"I don't think so, Pio. And that officer who is investigating Manuel's death—Tom Riley—I think he's on the level."

"Sure, I know Riley."

He stood up suddenly and said, "Let's go." He started off through the trees at a swinging stride. He was shorter than I was, but he had always been one hell of a walker.

We were half an hour reaching Pio's nearest hide-out. It was a good one, on top of the ridge, with no approach that could not be covered by a good rifleman. Moreover, there were several escape routes, for the hide-out itself was a nest of boulders, moss-covered for the most part, in a cluster of stunted pines and cedars.

The escape routes were winding passages, almost like tunnels, among the boulders. There was a dripping spring— "About a gallon an hour," Pio commented. Two of the boulders were canted enough to offer a fair shelter for not more than two men; down among the rocks at a lower level there was another hollow, a sort of cave formed by boulders that would have sheltered twenty.

"My grandfather told me of this place," Pio said. "The Apaches used it."

In the cave, which was perhaps thirty feet across, there was an opening at the top that was a dozen feet wide and was partly shielded by a gnarled cedar's limbs and leaning trunk. The walls in some parts of the cave were black with ancient cooking fires, and in some places there was some almost illegible Indian writing.

"Is this on the Wells ranch?"

"No . . . they don't even know. That Floyd, he won't go anywhere he can't ride a horse. Jimbo's a lazy one. I t'ink nobody comes here but me. The Old Ones, they know. Maybe somebody at Fort Apache knows.

"That Jimbo . . . he don't even walk. Colin, he used to walk when he was a boy—no more. None of them come up to the ridges."

He grinned slyly. "They not Indian like me. Indian walk on the mountains."

Chapter 9

Pio started a fire, then went down into a small dark cave and cut two steaks from a side of beef that hung there. He grinned slyly as he emerged. "Wells beef. You want?"

Without waiting for a reply he squatted by the fire and prepared to broil the beef. "You never have to worry about meat. Wells beef is good beef."

Seated beside the fire, I found myself dozing, resting at last. For the first time I realized how exhausted I was. There, under the warm sun and near the fire, my eyes closed. The heat soaked into my weary muscles until slowly the tension was gone.

"You int'rested in them Toomeys?"

My eyes opened. The steaks were done. "What do you know about them?" I asked.

"They come up the country with a herd of cows. My grandfather saw them come when he was a little boy. He was lyin' up on the mountain to watch. He figured he'd never seen so many cows in the world. They kept comin' and comin' like it was forever, and the cowhands let them spread out along the river where the grass was good. Then the hands rode up to the wagon and got down from their saddles—like they'd come home. There was good grass along the Verde that year. Local rains, falling at the right time.

"Up where grandfather was lyin' with two other boys they could smell the meat. They saw John Toomey turn his head and look up toward where they lay. They figured if he had seen them he was a canny one, but they lay quiet, curious like squirrels.

"John Toomey he stepped into the saddle and rode

86

his horse over to the foot of the slope. They didn't know whether to run or stay.

"John Toomey he called up to them to come down, and he put presents out there on the ground, a row of five or six things, and then he rode off a ways an' waited.

"They came down, all right. They came slow like deer or antelope, sizin' up something they didn't understand. They found a sack of tobacco on the ground and a small packet of salt, and a jack-knife . . . they'd never seen a fold-up knife before.

"He called out to them and told them to come back and bring their fathers—told them to say John Toomey wanted to smoke with them."

That, I remembered, had been in the journal. The Toomeys knew they could never live in that country without the friendship of the Indians; and besides, they had an idea in their heads, a good idea.

They had met with the Indians, and with the chiefs. They made them gifts, and they talked; and the upshot of it was that John Toomey had bought land from the Indians. Bought land with well-defined boundaries, and received a deed on a buckskin in Indian writing.

Nor was that the end. The Toomeys knew that the times were changing, and they had learned a good deal during the war, talking with Yankee soldiers who had been in business. They were shrewd enough to see that the old ways of settling on land in the West were on the way out. They wanted land, but they wanted a solid claim to it.

That was the real secret of those pages from the journal, for it not only told of the purchase from the Indians, but also told how Clyde Toomey had ridden south, found the last survivor of the Mexican family that once held a Spanish grant to this land, and bought his claim from him.

Pio knew a part of the story. He did not know that Clyde Toomey had bought the land again from the Mexican claimants. He only knew that Clyde had ridden away, and after some days had returned.

In the meantime, there had been trouble. Some of the hands—he did not know how many—had quit and drifted west. Two had been killed night-herding.

They had not been killed by Apaches, though the intention had been to make the others believe Apaches responsible.

"Was there a Wells in the outfit that killed them?" I asked.

"No Wells . . . the Wells name came later, by marriage. Teale's daughter married a Wells—Marvin Teale. He was the one who done it. He was a little man, but strong. He came from California. We heard the talk." He grinned at me. "Most Indians stand quiet, say nothing, hear plenty.

"Teale had had to leave California . . . murder, we heard. He had known Reese somewhere, and Reese had already been thinking about all that land and those cattle. Reese knew nothing about the purchase of the land, or why Clyde went to Tucson that time.

"Teale and Reese, they ambushed Clyde Toomey and two hands. Killed them and hid their bodies, then they brought in some outlaws from Tucson and Tubac . . . and they killed the rest. It was white man's trouble. The Apache had trouble of his own."

The Apaches were always around, in the mountains, in the valleys, and like all wild things, they were curious. From up on the ridges they would spend hours watching the actions of the white men—actions that from their viewpoint were peculiar. And there was little they did not see. The motives for such actions they did not know, but what happened they had known.

"What about Belle Dawson? Where does she stand in this?"

"There was a boy—a very young boy. When the fight was over, Bal Moore . . . he carried him off. Later he came back and claimed a half section—a grazing claim—in his name and the kid's. Him I knew. He was a tough old man."

"They said he was killed by Apaches."

"They always say that. Apaches liked him. He got a bullet into Teale once . . . tried to kill him, but Teale lived. After that they dry-gulched Bal."

The meat was done, and it was good. When we had finished our coffee I got up. In spite of the bit of sleep I'd had during the night, and the rest now, I was still tired. But there was no time now to rest any longer.

"I'm going to get Belle from them," I said.

"You gone on her?" Pio asked.

"It isn't that. They'll want to kill her. She knows too much now, and they can't afford to have her around. I just hope I'm not too late."

"If you like her, you keep her away from Jimbo."

He got up. "All right, Cap, I'm with you. Only I'm shooting for the record."

"Give yourself a chance, Pio. You're out of prison— you can stay out. Don't shoot unless you have to. You can help me, but leave that to me, and when the show-down comes I'll speak for you."

"Nobody'd believe you, Cap. Nobody at all. They know Pio—they know me, and they know how I'll feel, them killing Pete and Manuel."

"Reese killed Pete—Belle told me. The point is, Pio, if you get convicted for killing any one of them, they'll have made a clean sweep. Play it smart, stay with me, help me, but don't shoot unless we're backed into a corner."

He looked at me. He dug into his shirt pocket and took out square of tobacco and bit off a chunk. He had always been a chewer, even in Korea.

"All right, we'll see."

"Think about it Apache-style, Pio. You kill Colin, and he's out of it. But suppose we get Belle away from him? Then suppose we go into court and prove that he doesn't own all this land? Suppose we can go into court and prove that he killed Manuel, or conspired to have him killed? Which would hurt him worse?"

"Yeah," he agreed reluctantly. "Yeah, I see what you mean."

We went along the mountain toward the northwest, keeping to the high country as an Indian does, watching the trails below.

As we walked I thought of Doris. She was cold, and she liked violence. Belle would be in her greatest danger when in Doris' hands . . . perhaps even more so than in the hands of Jimbo, who was a spoiled boy who had never grown up, and one whose strength as well as his wealth had given him all he'd ever wanted.

Never in my life had I sought out a fight, but I'd never lagged much when the time for one came. Perhaps I am a throw-back to some earlier, less law-abiding era. There is no one anywhere who has more respect for the law or for men of the law who do a hard job well, when they do it honestly—and most of them are honest. But now we were for the time being beyond the reach of the law. There was one chance in a hundred that my call had gotten through, that the operator was curious enough or concerned enough to inform the police.

The police might dismiss it as one of the many freakish things that do happen. On the other hand, good police officers have a sense of impending trouble, and a natural inclination to be not only suspicious, but skeptical. Their work, and the people they meet in the course of the day's work, make them so. They know, for instance, that some drivers will lie when stopped for a traffic violation, and as many will ignore traffic regulations if they believe they can get away with it. And often enough a boy who disrespects the law has learned it in the front seat of a car, watching his father, or listening to him try to alibi himself out of a ticket.

There was a good chance that the police had their own ideas about Colin and Jimbo Wells. They might just drive down to the ranch to check on the telephone call— if it ever got through.

In another few minutes we saw them. They were a thousand feet below us and about a quarter of a mile out on the flat, headed for the headquarters ranch.

Belle was with them. She was sitting her horse, her

hands tied behind her, and her horse on a lead-rope to Colin Wells' horse. They were all there, in a tight little group. Off ahead of them was a jeep, which we saw through the telescopic sight on Pio's rifle. But it was in evidence chiefly by its dust cloud.

They must have finished out the night on Seward's Bar-Bell ranch, and started out early for the home ranch. I had an idea that Benton Seward had hastened their going . . . he would be worried about that phone call and would want them far enough away so he could claim that he knew nothing about any of it.

Where we were we had cover enough to remain unseen, but they must have been worried about us. They knew I was out here somewhere, and that I constituted a threat in every sense. They also knew there was at least one other man, and no doubt they had decided that it was Pio Alvarez.

It was just past noon when we hunched down among the junipers on the slope of the Mustang Hills just above Tangle Creek. We were about two miles from the ranch house, but in a good position to see what went on.

Pio had not spoken a word since we left the hide-out on Cedar Mountain. He had lost none of his skill at moving across broken ground, and it was easy to see why the Apache had always preferred to fight on foot. They might ride a horse to the scene of action, but they fought on the ground. Pio possessed an instinctive feeling for terrain; he kept to low ground, utilizing every bit of cover, alert to every sound.

Neither of us needed to be told we were getting close to a showdown. Belle Dawson was down there and we had to get her away. I was hoping it could be done without bloodshed, for this was no longer the West of the days when bloodshed was taken for granted. When a man was wounded or killed nowadays, people asked for explanations, and coroners' juries investigated.

How many of the Wells riders would stand for killing or injuring a woman? Rough as they were, and willing as they had proved themselves to kill rustlers, I doubted if any of them—unless it might be Reese—would stand by while harm came to a woman. Especially if it was one whom they all knew and had no reason to dislike.

Pio kept taking sights on the ranch, picking out each bit of movement and studying it through his telescopic sight. It worried me. When might he decide to shoot? Of course, we were too far off, and he could see little, distinguishing those he knew by some manner or movement or by the clothes we had seen them wear earlier.

After a brief rest we skirted the edge of the hills, and within an hour we were among the rocks and brush behind the ranch house. Below us the pool was a splash of deep blue, the white house a picture of comfort. Benton Seward's jeep stood in the open near the house.

How many were down there? Colin, Jimbo, Mark Wilson, and Seward? How about Reese?

As we watched, a man came to the bunkhouse door and looked around. He was wearing a belt gun. He walked slowly toward the corral, pausing from time to time to look about him.

"Rip Parker," Pio muttered. "He's a bad one. So's Dad Styles. Both of them were on the spot when Pete was killed. Pete had trouble with Rip over in Prescott one time. Parker whupped him pretty bad."

We waited, watching the ranch, sleeping by turns, but we saw nothing of Belle, nor of Doris.

In mid-afternoon Mark Wilson came out, got into the jeep, and drove off down the road toward the mountains. Except for this, the place seemed lifeless. There was no sign of a police car. My call must have failed, then, and there was no other chance to reach a telephone.

While Pio slept, I left our vantage point and, while staying within viewing distance of the ranch, succeeded in scouting the terrain behind us. First I looked for a way of escape if we were located. I found two partially covered routes by which we could get away from the slope. One was a deep draw, the other was sheltered by cedars.

The lack of movement down there at the ranch worried me. They had no choice now but to find and kill us, so why weren't they trying? As the day wore on, I became increasingly jumpy, starting at the slightest sound. Out in lonely country there are always such sounds—the rustle of some small animal moving, the trickle of sand, the sound of wind, however slight.

Without a doubt we were being hunted. Even as we lay here men would be searching for us, men who knew this terrain, men who could guess our objectives, who would know where to look. We might choose to escape, or we might choose to pull Belle out of trouble. In either case they would be ready for us. It was not a comfortable thought to realize that they might come upon us at any time. Yet there was no sign of them, no sound of them.

With the coming of twilight Pio was awake. He listened as I whispered to him of my scouting, and mentioned the two routes of escape.

With the approach of darkness Dad Styles came from the bunkhouse and relieved Rip Parker, who went inside, probably to eat.

"All right," I said suddenly, "let's go."

We started down the rocky slope, working our way with care. The ranch house lay before us, and we were intent upon reaching it without arousing any excitement there. We had moved quietly but steadily, our concern directed at the house, and at the dark figure of Dad Styles. So intent were we with moving silently and watching Styles for any sign of alarm that we were caught flat-footed when three flashlights suddenly held us in their glare.

"All right." Colin's triumph trembled in his tone. "Drop the guns."

My only wonder is that they did not shoot us down where we stood.

There was simply no chance for us. At least four shotguns and as many rifles covered us at close range.

We had been fools not to think they would be waiting for us on the slope, and we had walked right into the trap. It had all been too neat, too easy. We had worried about what lay above and behind us, and we had worried about the ranch house. We had not given a thought to that slope below us and within range of our eyes, yet it was the logical, natural route for anyone wanting to approach the house under cover.

We dropped our guns and lifted our hands.

Pio didn't turn his head, but suddenly he chuckled. It was an old, familiar sound, and I knew what it meant. "Well, keed," he said mildly, "here we go again."

"What's he mean?" Seward asked nervously. "What's he saying?"

"Nothing," Colin replied impatiently. "For God's sake, Bent, relax. It's all over now. We've got them and we've got Belle. Now we can close the book."

"You're very naive, Wells," I said casually, "if you think this book can be closed. If anything happens to us you'll have kicked up a nest of hornets. I'm expected in Los Angeles, and my publisher is a very nervous man. If I don't show up he'll start wiring everybody in the country . . . he's done it before when less money was involved."

"So what?"

"So he wires the sheriff, he wires the governor, he wires the attorney general. He's hell on wheels when he gets going."

"Huh!" Jimbo snorted. "You aren't all that important."

"Money is important to everybody, and I represent money to a lot of people."

We went ahead, Pio a step or two in front of me, walking carefully. They had us, and they were very sure of it. But desperate as the situation was, I couldn't lose hope. I suppose one never does, really. Books and motion pictures have prepared us for rescue . . . only this wasn't any motion picture.

"Colin," I heard Seward protest in a whisper, "we're running a big risk. After all, he's a pretty well-known man. Sheridan isn't just a rustler."

"And this isn't a few head of beef, either," Colin

replied shortly. "It's everything we own, your ranch and mine. What more could we lose?"

At the ranch house lights were on in the living room and the play room. Doris was having a drink, and the radio was playing softly; it was a setting completely out of tune with the situation. Doris looked across her glass at me and smiled.

"Well, well! Look who's here!"

"It was you," I said. "I just couldn't stay away. I kept remembering how you looked in that bathing suit."

She laughed, but the expression in her eyes was cool, calculating. This was a girl with a mind like a computer, and at the center of it but one thought: *What's good for Doris?*

She was the strongest, Benton the weakest of them all; and if we had a chance it would come from one or the other of them. If somehow we could make Benton Seward more afraid of what might come from our deaths than from what might happen if we did not die, we might save ourselves. On the other hand, if we were to try to work on Doris, we would have to convince her that her only sure way of winning was if we lived.

"I want a drink," Seward said, and went over to the bar.

Mark Wilson looked after him irritably, then exchanged a glance with Colin.

"How soon is supper?" Colin asked Doris. "I'm hungry."

"It won't be long." She looked over at me. "Now you've got him, what are you going to do with him?"

Nobody wanted to say it. They were all thinking it, but nobody wanted actually to use the words. Pio sensed it, too, and grinned.

"Better'n Korea," he said to me. "Warmer, anyway."

Seward looked around. "What's that mean? What's between you two?"

"We were in Korea together." I sat back on my chair. "We escaped together. We were captured, and we escaped again."

"That greaser was a soldier?" Jimbo asked.

"And a good one," I said. "A first-class fighting man. By actual count he killed twenty-seven Red Chinese during our escape."

They looked at me, and then at him, but they did not believe it.

"Him?" Jimbo sneered.

"Bully boy," I said, "Pio could take you in an alley and ruin you. You never saw the day you could handle one side of him. He can invent more dirty fighting on the spur of the moment than you've heard of in all your life."

"Maybe we'll see," Jimbo said belligerently. "Maybe we'll go out in the corral and see."

"If you're going to give out any favors," I said, "let me have the first chance."

"You?" He stared at me.

"Me," I said.

"I'd like to see that," Doris said. "I really would." And she meant it.

"There'll be none of that," Colin said. "Now shut up and let's get something to eat."

Seward toyed with his glass, his expression sour. He had hoped to avoid this, to be somewhere else when it happened—whatever it was that was going to happen. He was a frightened man.

Mark Wilson had drifted out of the room, and I heard him outside giving directions to some cowhands. Most of the ones who could not be relied on to keep their mouths shut were no doubt out at line shanties by this time. The hands who were on the place would be the tough and tested ones. Wilson would be posting guards.

Why had they not killed us at once? Was there still someone around who might have heard what was going on? Or had they some other plan in mind?

And where was Belle?

"A good poker player," I suggested suddenly, "throws in his hand when he doesn't have the cards; and when the cards run against him he'll cash in and get out of the game—if he's smart."

"Only you can't cash in," Jimbo said. "You haven't anything to cash."

Doris was looking at me thoughtfully, and I said, "Some men can take prison; no woman can. Not if she wants to remain beautiful."

After a minute I added, "No matter what happens here tonight, nothing will ever be the same again. It will be months before the investigation ends, and at the end of it a lot of doors will be closed; so even if you win, you lose.

"Right from the first," I continued, "it was a plan that was full of holes. There were so many things you didn't know. You assumed I was a city boy who wouldn't be at home on a horse. If there was an accident, you thought nobody would be surprised. As a matter of fact, everybody who knows me, and a lot of people who just know about me, would be surprised. They all know that I can ride.

"From the first, this business was planned with no careful thought, no real understanding. You thought killing me would end the matter, but that would only be the beginning.

"By now Riley will have established the connection between Pio and me. Our story received a good bit of attention at the time, and the information is in both our records.

"During an interview I mentioned the Toomeys. By this time Riley knows that, and that will lead him here. So, if Pio and I are gone, you'd better have some good explanations. Of course, they won't do any good, but even if they did, even if you come out of this unscathed, how long will it be before Dad Styles, Rip Parker, or Floyd starts getting notions. So after you kill us, who do you kill next?"

"Shut up," Colin said. "You talk too much."

The room was silent. Doris Wells was, if I read her

correctly, a woman completely concerned with herself —her beauty, her comforts, her pleasures. I had no doubt that had things gone well she would have been content to live out her life with Colin; but what I hoped to do was to convince her that this was a sinking ship, and that her one chance of saving herself was to free Pio and myself.

Ice rattled in a glass as Bent Seward fixed himself another one.

Mark Wilson stuck his head in the door. "Soup's on," he said, and disappeared. Jimbo got up and stretched, then started for the door. Nobody else moved.

"By now," I said, as if talking to myself, "my secretary is calling the motel. She won't have received the next tape and she will be worried."

"Let's get Belle in here and get it over with," Colin said, but he did not move.

They had not tied either of us, but now, with Doris holding the gun, they did so. Colin did the tying, with Benton watching sourly.

Then Doris and Colin went into the next room. We heard the subdued rattle of dishes, followed by quiet. Bent Seward was sitting down, drinking.

"No need for you to get caught in the middle," I said; "this wasn't your idea."

"They goin' to be worried about you," Pio said.

"Don't be silly," Seward said, trying to appear confident.

"You could get out of this," I said. "You could turn us loose."

"Are you kidding?"

"By this time my secretary is calling my publisher. He should be in Denver today. She will tell him she hasn't heard from me and is worried." This was unlikely, but knowing Marie, I knew it was possible. "My publisher is a nervous man, and he will be worried too. He and the governor were fraternity brothers. By midnight the State Highway Police will be making inquiries."

Seward was sweating. He looked at the floor, then

slumped back in his chair, staring at the ice in his empty glass.

Pio hitched himself to the edge of the sofa. He was looking at the table. My eyes followed his to the cigarette lighter.

"You could get out of this, Seward," I said again. "You could turn us loose, get in your car, and drive off. As far as that goes, you could drive us to the capital."

"We wouldn't get off the place. He will have the gates closed and guarded, long ago."

"Leave that to us," Pio said.

Just then Colin thrust his head in the door. "You'd better get something to eat, Bent," he said. "We're going to take care of this right after breakfast."

"What about us?" I asked.

He ignored me, and closed the door behind him.

I looked at Seward again. "Well, there it is," I said. "You can't procrastinate much longer. And if you don't eat," I added softly, "somebody else might; and they would get the break from the law for helping us."

He stood up and started to speak, then turned and walked out of the room.

"Well," Pio said, "we tried."

We had tried, and all that we had said was likely to be true. The trouble was, it would happen too late. I didn't think they had any chance of getting away with it, but they were moving ahead as if unable to stop, and we were going to be killed.

The fact that it would prove to be a useless crime wasn't going to help us in the least. We would be dead.

Chapter 10 ᴧᴧᴧᴧᴧᴧᴧᴧᴧᴧᴧᴧᴧᴧᴧᴧᴧᴧᴧᴧᴧᴧᴧᴧᴧ

The door opened and Jimbo came back into the room. The moment he looked at me I knew what he had come for. He held a sandwich in one hand and he was chewing a large bite of it. In the other hand he held a beer. He put the mug down on a table and looked at me, and then at Pio. Carefully, then, he put the sandwich down beside it and walked across the room.

He lifted his heavy hand and slapped me across the mouth.

I just looked at him, not saying a word. That seemed to infuriate him, and he turned my chin gently with his fingers and drew back his right fist. As he started the punch, with legs spread, Pio fell over on the floor behind him. I slipped the punch by moving my head, then using my braced feet, shot myself off the sofa. My skull took him in the mid-section and he toppled back over Pio.

He struck the floor, his head hitting hard, and Pio threw himself across Jimbo's legs. I had lunged after him, and falling, dug my knee into his throat. He squirmed and grunted, but we had our dead weight on him and he could not throw us off.

Suddenly the door opened behind us. "Jimbo—"

It was Colin. I caught the startled expression on his face, and then he was running toward us. Grabbing me by the collar, he gave me a jerk, but I fell against him as Jimbo rolled free, and as Jimbo got up Pio lunged at him and sank his teeth into his neck.

Jimbo ripped him off and threw him to the floor, then rushed at me, aiming a wild kick at my head. I was on my knees, so I threw myself against his leg and knocked him off balance. He staggered, and Colin gave me a shove toward the sofa.

Jimbo's face was white with rage. He started for me, but Colin grabbed him. "Stop, you fool! *Stop it, I say!*"

A trickle of blood ran from the side of Jimbo's neck where Pio had bitten him, and his eyes were glazed with a wild, unreasoning fury.

Violently, he threw Colin off and came for me again, but at that instant the phone rang. At the sharp jangle of sound everyone froze into immobility.

Jimbo stared wildly, startled into awareness. As Colin reached for the phone the door opened and Doris appeared. "Let me have that!" she said.

"Doris!" It was a shrill, unpleasant feminine voice that came over the wire. "Doris Wells, where *have* you been? I've been trying to get you for *ages!* We tried all afternoon, and I just can't imagine you all being out at one time! Esther and Andy are over here, and we thought if you didn't mind we'd run over for a dip, and—"

"I'm afraid it's out of the question tonight. We—"

"But we wouldn't *disturb* you! We'd just come over for a dip, and—"

"Call the police!" I interrupted. My voice was clear. "Call them right now, whoever you are! Call Detective Tom Ri—"

For a moment no one reacted to my words—but only for a moment. Then Colin threw himself at me, and grabbed my throat in his hands.

But even as his hands grasped my throat, I was rolling with the movement, and he went over onto the floor, and I jerked my knees up into his belly.

Doris slammed the telephone down. "You *fools!*" she was screaming. "Can't you do anything *right!*"

Colin Wells got up off the floor. He took time to brush himself off. He was suddenly in command. "Doris," he said, "get some highball glasses in here. I want three or four of them half empty. I want half-smoked cigarettes . . . several of them . . . in all the ash trays. I want it to look as if we've been having a party.

"And then I want you to get Belle. We'll settle this matter right here and now."

Pio lay where he had been thrown, but his eyes were on me, bright and hard. He seemed to be trying to say something to me.

Doris got busy, arranging the room. Then she went out, and it was only a few minutes until she returned with Belle Dawson. There was a welt on Belle's cheekbone and a small cut on her jaw. She had been struck hard, more than once.

But when she looked over at us, she smiled, and I grinned back at her.

Colin wasted no time. "Belle, we're buying you out." He placed a sheet of paper before her on the table. "Sign here."

"I'll do nothing of the sort," she said calmly.

"You haven't any choice, Belle, none whatsoever. We've waited too long for this, and we will wait no longer."

"Don't give them anything, Belle," I said. "They are murderers who come from a long line of murderers. All you see here is founded on cattle and land stolen from your family."

Colin waited me out, and then said simply, "All that is no longer important. Sign this paper and we will let you go."

They had come up close to Belle, intent on her and the paper.

My eyes went to Doris. She stood at one side, and she was not looking at Belle, but at me. I knew what she was thinking. That telephone call had been the second call for help, this one from the Wells ranch instead of the Seward place. And this one was almost sure to have been heard.

I had no idea who the woman on the other end of the line had been, but my hunch was that she was a talkative one who even now was exclaiming over what she had heard. She might even call the police, and she had sounded the sort who in the event of an investigation would be only too willing to talk on the witness stand.

Doris seemed hesitant, and I had an idea that she had given up on Colin. Now she was thinking of how she could come out of this and not lose everything. Suggestively, I lifted my hands, bound together at the wrists.

Doris deliberately walked around the table and stood beside me and then edged past me. As she did so, she thrust something into my fingers, which I concealed. . . . A nail file.

"Colin," Doris said now, "there isn't time for that

now. If I know Hazel, she will be on her way over here. Get them out. Hide them until she's gone."

He looked at her, obviously considering what she had said. "A good idea. We'll take them out to the old fort. The walls are thick enough and it is far enough out so that nobody will hear anything from there, and Belle can sign a paper there as well as here."

We were jerked to our feet and shoved, half running, through the door and across the yard. Rip Parker was standing in front of the bunkhouse, and he looked at me with an ironic grin. I saw that much as they pushed me past the lighted door.

At the old fort the heavy plank door was opened and we were thrust inside.

"Think about it, Belle," Colin said. "We'll be back as soon as we can get things straightened up."

And then they were gone.

For a moment we neither moved nor spoke. I had no illusions as to what would happen when Belle had signed that paper—or for that matter, what would happen if she did not sign it.

For all our skill at guerilla fighting we had walked into a trap and had been taken like a pair of youngsters. And now we were tied up and waiting for the slaughter.

Doris had gone as far as she would go. She had given me the nail file, and had intended this move as a chance to use it. Now she had an out. If all failed and she was brought to trial, she would be able to say she had been afraid to go against her husband, but had done the best she could in supplying me with a means to escape. She had what she wanted, an extenuating circumstance . . . and no doubt she didn't really care whether we got away or not.

Edging close to Pio, I whispered, "I've got a nail file."

"Take a long time," he muttered.

Pushing it into his fingers, I said, "Work on it. I've got another idea."

It was dark inside the fort, with the musty smell of a

place long closed. "Belle, have you ever been in this place before? What's been stored here?"

"Odds and ends of broken harness, an old saddle or two, some grain sacks . . . mostly junk."

There was a padlock on the outside of the door. I had heard them snap it shut, and that door was heavy plank, reinforced inside and out by cross pieces. Even if we freed ourselves we were still locked in, and the walls were stone, and they were thick and strong.

Whatever they planned to do to us would be done soon, I felt sure. They could not afford to wait, nor could they afford to create suspicion. There had probably been too much of that already, and they had been guilty of overconfidence and clumsiness.

Yet when it began it must have seemed from their viewpoint an easy matter. I would be an invited guest, they had no motive for wanting me out of the way that anyone could guess . . . it would simply be an accident. I was a city boy trying to ride a horse on mountain trails. They had not guessed that I was an experienced rider, and they had not considered the role that Pio would play.

What I was going to try now was something I could have done with ease ten years before, but I had always been active, I was limber enough, and I had an idea I could do it now.

In tying my wrists they had tied them tightly enough right above the hands. Any higher and I would have had no chance to do what I planned. Moreover, I had narrow hips, which would be a help.

Getting up to my knees, I lowered the loop of my arms as far as possible, then started to back my hips through the loop. My arms were long for my height, but it was a struggle. After several minutes of trying I managed it, and now had my hands behind my knees. Rolling on my back and drawing my knees up under my chin, I put my feet through the loop of my arms and had my wrists in front of me.

Streaming with perspiration, I sat and gasped for several minutes, and then I began to work on the knots with my teeth. In a matter of minutes, I was free.

Moving to Pio, who had already cut partly through his ropes, I simply broke the rope and untied him, and then untied Belle.

"So now where are we?" Pio said. "And even if we break out of here, there'll be a guard."

Just then we heard a car coming along the trail, then into the ranch yard. As the headlights swept over the fort a little light came through the narrow firing slots and gave me a quick chance to see what lay around us.

Junk was the word Belle had used to describe the contents, and there were odds and ends of harness, some worn boots, an old McClellan saddle, obviously unused for many years, a wooden bucket half filled with the bits and pieces that accumulate around any working ranch and are rummaged through from time to time in making repairs. These probably included nuts, bolts, screws, rusty hinges.

"Cap," Pio said suddenly, "let's try the roof."

The roof? I tried to recall what the journal had said about the roof. Had it said anything at all?

"Belle, what is the roof? Is it stone or timber or what?"

She was silent for a moment and then she said, "Dan, I'm sorry to say I don't know. I must have walked or ridden past it a hundred times, but I don't remember."

"Gimme a boost, Cap," Pio said.

Reaching out in the dark, I touched his shoulder, then clasped my hands for his boot. He felt for my hands to locate them, and put his foot in the stirrup they made. I lifted and he gave a jump so that he was able to touch the roof.

"Logs," he said, "split logs." He strained for a moment, and dust sifted down over my shoulders. "Dirt on top."

He stepped down. "What d' you think, Cap?"

"Old logs . . . if any nails were used they would have rusted . . . they'd be loose, unless the roof has been rebuilt."

"They might squeak."

"We'll risk it," I said. "If the guard is close by he'll probably hear it and come to stop us; if he isn't, we've got a chance to get out."

"Like in Korea, that time?"

"Uh-huh. Get on my shoulders," I said. "If you get your shoulders under a weak board, we can both push."

We had no luck. We started at one side and tested our strength, but either the dirt was piled too deep, or the nails were still gripping. We moved over, tried again, and then a third time. We worked our way along, testing each board, each foot of the roof.

Suddenly there was a glare of light. Pio dropped to the floor. "What's that?" he whispered.

Belle was at one of the loop holes. "The lights at the swimming pool. Hazel is really going to swim."

"It's cold out there," I said.

"It's a heated pool, Dan." She watched for a moment. "Esther Karnes is with her, and if I know those two they won't leave until they know what's going on. I never thought I'd see the day when I'd be glad they were close by. There aren't two women in all of Arizona it is easier to dislike."

"Why do they have them over, then?"

"Esther Karnes," Belle said, "is the sister of a county commissioner. She's also very active politically."

A boot grated on gravel near the door, and we waited, keeping our silence, listening. After a while the steps retreated, and we immediately went back to testing the roof. All at once a rusty spike squealed and we held our breath.

Outside we heard running footsteps, which paused just outside. Pio's lips at my ear breathed, "I can make it, Cap! One more time!"

The boots prowled around the stone fort, then retreated slowly.

"Now?" I said.

"Why not?"

I gave him a leg up. He braced his shoulders. "On three," he whispered, and I readied myself, knees bent.

"One, two, three!" We both heaved, and the board lifted. There was a trickle of dirt, a rattle of pebbles on the floor; then we saw the dark sky through a rectangle of opening, a dark sky spangled with stars. Cool air blew into the fort.

Pio caught the edge, and eased himself up through the narrow space. For me there would have to be a larger opening.

Pio thrust his head back through the hole. "You can make it, ma'am. He can't."

"Go ahead," I said to Belle. "I'll make a bigger opening."

"How will you get up that high?"

"I can jump and catch the edges. You go ahead now."

She wasted no time. I helped her up, and Pio pulled her through the narrow space.

"Pio, get her away from here . . . clear away."

He chuckled. "Sure, keed!"

He was feeling the edges of the hole we'd made. One of the logs had split, probably around the rusting spike, and so had been easily pushed out of place. Apparently he was trying to move one of the other logs.

"Don't bother with that!" I said. "Beat it!"

There was no sense in having them caught again. If they could get away, get help . . . even stir up enough talk so an investigation would be started . . .

Something sounded outside the door . . . boots on the gravel again. "You keep quiet in there," a voice said in a hoarse whisper, "or I'll come in an' give you the butt of this gun in the teeth."

Suddenly there was a grunt, a gasp, then a moment of wild struggle. Heels beat against the wall, then the beating grew feeble . . . and then silence.

A head appeared at the opening above. "Jus' like in Korea, Cap. I'll open the door."

When the door opened I stepped outside. Pio and I

together picked up the unconscious man and took him inside. At least, I hoped he was only unconscious. Knowing Pio, I could not be sure.

"Here." Pio thrust a gun and cartridge belt into my hand. "I've got the rifle."

When we had closed and locked the door from the outside, I looked around. "Where's Belle?"

He gave a little chuckle. "She's got nerve, that one. She's gone up there." He gestured toward the pool.

"What?"

"She's going to tell Hazel the whole story. Right in front of them. And she's going to ask for a ride into town."

The sheer nerve of it stopped me, but then I recalled all that had happened. "They won't let her go, Pio. They've gone beyond that. Or if she got away, they would claim she was suffering from hysteria."

As we stood there together, wondering what to do, we could see her dark, slim figure walking along. She was almost at the pool. Walking on cat feet, we followed.

Doris was there by the pool in a white bikini, and Colin too.

Nobody ever had more nerve than Belle. She stepped out of the darkness and Colin jumped as if he'd been shot.

"Hazel, will you give me a ride into town?" Belle asked. "I must leave right away."

"We've only just started swimming," Hazel protested. "I've just gotten my suit wet."

"I must go right away," Belle insisted.

"Don't be silly, Belle," Colin said casually. "Let them have their swim. I know you've been restless lately, but you're much better off right here." He was thinking fast—I'll give him that. "We'll take care of you right here. You've no reason to go to a hospital . . . of any kind."

Hazel reached for her robe, and Esther Karnes caught the ladder and climbed out of the pool. "What's the trouble?"

"Belle's been rather nervous lately," Colin said gently. "I'm afraid she's been under a strain since her sister died, and she's not quite herself."

"My sister did not die," Belle said. "She was murdered. Just as you would like to murder me . . . and Dan Sheridan."

"Dan Sheridan? The writer?" Esther Karnes was excited. "Why, he's a favorite of Dick's!"

Colin got up. He seemed to have changed his mind, and his manner was quite unconcerned.

"Hazel, why don't you just do as she wishes? Humor her. It will do no harm. Drive her into town . . . just see that she doesn't harm herself."

Belle stared at him, and my mind went blank with surprise. "You don't mean it!" she exclaimed.

"Of course I mean it. Hazel, it would be doing us all a favor if you would. That was one reason we hesitated when you wanted to come out. We had a party here last night and some of the guests started calling people . . . long distance, and at my expense . . . and saying all sorts of crazy things.

"Why, we haven't done that since we were kids! Remember when we used to call perfect strangers in the middle of the night? You would think they had outgrown that. I'll admit," he added, "it was Jimbo who started it, but—"

"That's not true!" Belle interrupted. "He's lying!"

"Belle got a bit excited and she began believing all sorts of things . . . people trying to kill her, and things like that. As for killing her sister—my own brother Aukie was killed, too, you know."

He was good, I had to admit that, and I had not believed he had it in him. He was smoothing it all over and giving a very good portrayal of a considerate man.

"If I were you, Hazel, and if Esther doesn't mind, I'd take her into town before she changes her mind."

"Has he gone nuts?" Pio whispered. "If she ever gets into town and tells what she knows he'll have the Law all over the place out here!"

"Why, of course!" Hazel said. "I'd be only too glad to help. Belle, you poor thing! You just sit down and we'll get dressed and be right along."

They disappeared and Belle said quietly, "What do you hope to gain by that? You know nobody will believe it." She got up to go inside, and as she started Colin spoke again.

"Of course they will. Now you just go along with Hazel," he said. "There's nothing to worry about."

Jimbo had remained silent up to now. "Colin," he said, "you just can't mean to let her go."

"Oh, but I do!" He sounded cheerful. "This is working out beautifully." He turned around. "Mark, is Seward's jeep still out back?"

"It is." Mark just stood there, waiting.

"You know the old fire road that runs into the highway near Bishop Creek? If you were to leave now, you could be parked up there with your lights out."

Mark Wilson took a pack of cigarettes from his pocket and shook one loose. He took time to light it, and said something too indistinctly for me to hear.

"It will look better that way. No lights, mind you, and no contact."

They talked some more, but I couldn't quite make out what they were saying, only a word or two coming through.

We backed off, and when safely beyond their hearing, I said to Pio, "What about that old fire road? Do you know where it is?"

"Uh-huh."

"I don't understand what he has in mind. Why would he let them leave the place if he intends to take them again? And why so far away? That's off the ranch, isn't it?"

"Sure."

"What's up there? On that old fire road?"

"Nothin'. Nothin' a-tall. There was a brush fire up yonder a few years back and they had that fire road cut in . . . it's more of a fire break. Rough to go over, even on a horse."

We waited in silence, watching the house. Mark Wilson

and Jimbo disappeared. We heard a motor come to life, then Jimbo returned and said something to Colin.

When Belle came out again she was walking quietly beside Hazel. The three women got into Hazel's station wagon, and Colin stood quietly by, watching them drive away.

"Cap, we got to get out of here. Sooner or later somebody's goin' to have a look at the fort."

I got up and led the way toward the fort. We circled it, then paused. "I don't like it, Pio. Something's wrong. Colin's not going to let her get into town and do any talking. He doesn't dare."

"Well, he's let her go."

A thought came to me. "Pio, what's it like up there? I mean up there where that fire road runs into the main road."

"It's pretty rough country. And right there . . . I wouldn't want to drive that fire road in the dark, believe me. Right where it turns into the main road . . . I'd say he'd better make that turn. If he doesn't it's two hundred feet, straight down for him."

"Or for anybody driving the main road," I said. "Suppose somebody comes roaring down from the fire road out of the dark, what would you do?"

"I'd step on it."

"If it was a surprise? Mightn't you swing away?"

"I wouldn't dare. There's that drop-off, Cap. There just ain't room to swing away. On that narrow road if you twist your wheel you'll go over. Really good brakes, if you slapped them hard and quick, might catch you, but I wouldn't bet on it."

"That's it, then. He's planning to kill all three of them. If all three die there's not likely to be any suspicion that it was aimed at Belle."

"It's crazy."

Within me there was a sudden vast emptiness. Belle was going to die, and I had stood by and let her go. All I had thought of was that she would be off the ranch, in the company of other people, women Colin would not dare offend, and whose suspicion he would not dare arouse.

It hadn't occurred to me that he might kill all three of them to get at Belle. And now there was nothing I could do.

Chapter 11 ᴬᴬᴬᴬᴬᴬᴬᴬᴬᴬᴬᴬᴬᴬᴬᴬᴬᴬᴬᴬᴬᴬᴬ

Pio started off and I followed. Once, glimpsing the road, I saw the car's lights some distance off, headed south.

"Why are they going south?"

"Cap, that road takes a big bend. Don't you remember when you drove in here? You see the ranch from the top of the pass, but the road has to swing clear around the mountain."

I grabbed him. "Pio! Is there any way over that mountain? I mean, could we get there first?"

"Horses!" He started to run.

Suddenly I remembered that most of the saddle stock was kept in a lower corral, down in the valley and away from the ranch. Horses were brought up to the upper corral only when somebody was planning to ride.

We had ridden past that corral when starting for the mountains, and I had seen the horses. There was a cabin there, too, I remembered.

Pio slowed down, breathing hard. "There'll be a man in the cabin, won't there?" I asked.

He turned his face toward me in the dark. "Floyd Reese lives there. He and Dad Styles."

We crept up to the corral in the dark. There was a shed where the saddles were kept. Pio caught up a rope and walked swiftly to the corral and ducked between the bars, leaving his rifle beside the gate.

The horses moved away, but the rush of their feet halted, and then I heard Pio say softly, "Got him!"

A light went on in the cabin. The horses stampeded across the corral again, worried by this strange man who came to them at night, and without a lantern.

The door opened and a man came out, carrying an electric lantern. It was Dad Styles, and he was walking right toward me. Abruptly he stopped.

"Who's there?"

"Just keep walking, Styles. Just walk right past me. I don't want to kill you."

"Why, you're that damn' four-flushin' writer!"

He threw the lantern at me, and I saw the light glint on a gun as he jerked it from his waistband. I drew and fired. He folded in the middle and went to his knees, and I walked up and kicked the gun away from his hand. As I did so flame stabbed the night from the bunkhouse door, and throwing myself to my right, I fired as I hit the ground. I missed, and fired again.

The bullet hit something—the door jamb, I thought—and in the shadows beyond the rays of light from the fallen electric lantern, I saw Reese dart from the door. I gave him a lead, then fired.

He hit the ground skidding, and swung the rifle past me, aiming toward the corral. I took my time, lined up on the spot where he seemed to be, and fired a split second before he did.

The stab of flame lanced the night, at an angle too high. I fired again, and from the corral Pio fired.

A shout came from the house, and somebody was running.

Pio came up, leading two saddled horses. I swung into the leather and wheeled the horse, and as I did so, Floyd Reese raised up from the ground with a pistol held in both hands. Chopping down with the gun, I fired, shooting right down into his chest at point-blank range.

I tried another shot, turning as I did so, but the gun clicked on an empty chamber.

Pio was leading off at a dead run, and from behind us came rifle shots, but they were futile shots, for we were beyond several obstacles and well into the darkness.

Pio turned off the road suddenly and went up a rocky bank and through the brush and cedars. There was no visible trail that I could see, although desert trails usually show white in the darkness. Following closely, I shucked shells from the cartridge belt and reloaded the pistol, wishing I had a rifle.

Pio rode swiftly, seeming to have eyes like a cat. He picked his way among boulders, slid down the bank of a wash, scrambled his horse up the opposite side, and then went into a lope along the long slope of a hill. There was no sign of the car, although once when the horses slowed to pick their way down a steep declivity, I thought I heard the sound of a motor.

Wilson must have started his motor, then coasted the jeep away from the house until he could start up and edge away so they would not know he was leaving.

It was not difficult to imagine the scene as Colin planned it. The three women . . . Hazel, who was rather high-strung, to say the least, at the wheel. They would be talking, Hazel and Esther concerned about the girl between them, and Belle trying to make them realize what had actually happened back at the ranch. There would be no other cars on that road, and they would be concerned with their conversation.

As I saw the picture, headlights would suddenly flare upon them from above and a car would come charging down off the mountain, only yards away. The instinctive reaction would be to swing the wheel to avert a crash . . . and there was no margin there, according to Pio.

A swing of the wheel . . . steep slope . . . and then a sheer drop. An awful crash followed by silence, perhaps by flames.

Mark Wilson would climb down at some convenient spot and make sure the job was finished; if it was not, he would finish it.

As long as they had us locked up, it would seem like the easiest way. They could take us out and be rid of us elsewhere, no doubt setting it up to make it appear that Pio, a known criminal, had killed me.

Only now we were free, and by now they must know it.

Pio pulled up to give the horses a breather. "How much farther?" I asked.

He pointed across the shallow valley before us at the black bulk of the mountain. The valley was a pool of blackness to the south, but there was starlight, and our eyes, accustomed to the night, could see quite clearly.

"The fire road's over there," he said.

He started his horse and I followed on. We could hear a car plainly now. It was the jeep, grumbling and growling as it rumbled over the rough terrain. Then the sound ceased.

The jeep was in position. The trap was set.

Suddenly we caught the gleam of headlights on the road below. The station wagon was coming along at a good clip.

We spurred our horses and rode at a break-neck pace over the mountain. We hit the road only yards in front of the station wagon, and as it skidded to a stop I jerked the car door open and pushed Hazel over.

She started to cry out, but I had already started the car. If we stopped now and explained they would never believe it. They had to see for themselves the trap into which they were driving.

"Colin planned to kill you all," I said. "Mark Wilson is waiting on the fire road with a jeep. He was going to push you off the mountain."

Belle gasped, but Hazel wasn't buying it. "Young man, whoever you are, I'll have you——"

The station wagon straightened out on a stretch, and ahead of me I saw the white place where the fire road came into the main road. I drove on, and just as we were a car's length from the fire road, I stepped down on the gas.

The station wagon leaped, headlights flared blindingly from our right and the jeep came off the mountain with a thunderous roar. My hands gripped hard on the wheel, my foot held the gas pedal down, and we shot past.

There was a rush and a roar behind us, a harsh grinding of gravel as Mark Wilson tried to make the turn . . . but I knew he had failed. As quickly as I could, I brought the station wagon to a halt, then backed up slowly.

Shakily, I got out. Over the rim there was a crackling of flames, a subdued explosion as the gas tank went, and then more crackling.

Pio stood there, rifle in hand. Even he was shaken. "He almost made it, Cap. He almost did."

Belle was there beside me, holding my arm in a grip so tight it almost hurt. Hazel came out from the car; she wasn't the fainting type.

"You must be Dan Sheridan. I've seen your picture. Was that really Mark Wilson? And to think of the times he's sat in my home! What's this all about, anyway?"

"It's the ranch," I said. "It really belongs to Belle. I was searching the story of the Toomey brothers and they were afraid I'd uncover the truth."

Pio rode closer. "Cap," he said, "they'll be hunting us."

"All right." I turned to Hazel. Talkative she might be, but there was iron in her, too. Esther Karnes had stayed in the car, shocked into silence. "Drive Belle into town, will you?" I said. "And report this to the authorities . . . particularly to Tom Riley, he's on the case."

"What are you going to do?" Belle asked.

"I'm going back to the ranch. To the old fort. There's something back there I have to get."

"Be careful. Colin will be furious."

"I don't think so. When he hears what happened he will call his lawyer, and he will start putting a case together. You'll see."

Turning toward the horse, I stopped. "You'd better have an ambulance sent out, and a doctor. I believe there's been some shooting."

"You *believe*?" Pio grinned at me. "You kiddin'?"

We took our time riding back to the ranch, and we stayed with the main road. All I could think of now was getting back to Los Angeles, but first I had to fulfill the last request of a dying cattleman, dead these ninety years.

He had written out the directions in the last of those

116

pages in the gun barrel—writing hastily added. They were, in effect, his last will and testament.

The ranch house was ablaze with lights when we rode into the yard. Leaving Pio with the horses, I got down and walked in.

Floyd Reese was lying on the floor and he was dead. Dad Styles, on the sofa, was bandaged up. He was pale, but he was alive, and judging by the look in his eyes, he would recover.

Doris was at the bar. She still wore the white bikini and she had a drink in her hand. There were dark hollows under her eyes.

Colin had a drink, too. Benton Seward was gone, as usual. "You, is it? Why have you come back?" Colin said.

"Mark missed," I said. "He went over the cliff."

He just looked at me.

"Belle's gone into town. She's sending a doctor. And the law."

He stared into his drink. "You've played hell," he said.

"It was you," I said. "If you hadn't invited me out here and tried to kill me, you might have gotten away with it."

Let him think that. He wouldn't have gotten away with it, of course. Not after I'd read the journal from the gun barrel. I would not have left it alone or forgotten it until I had worked it all out, and found the answers I wanted.

"It was your fault," he said; "a damned, nosy writer."

"I hope you won't forget anything," Doris commented. "I hope you remember it all."

She was referring to the nail file. She could make use of that idea now, just as she had planned. I'd be willing to bet that when the showdown came she'd get off scot-free.

"I'll not forget," I said, and backed away toward the door. I still had to go out to the old fort.

"Don't count your chickens." Colin looked up from his drink. "When all the cards are down, I'll still have the ranch. I'm in possession, and nobody but me has a thing to show."

"Cap look what I found." It was Pio in the doorway behind me.

Jimbo Wells was with him. "You take off that gun," he said, "and I'll take you apart."

He was big. He would outweigh me by a good bit. I remembered reading on some sports page that he weighed two hundred and sixty pounds, and he looked every bit of it.

But I had never liked Jimbo Wells. From the first moment I put eyes on him I had felt my hackles rising. He was rough and brutal in his own game, and he would be mean in a fight; but under whatever circumstances we met, Jimbo Wells and I would have fought, sooner or later. He knew it, and I knew it. He had the instincts of a bully, and I a deep-seated antagonism toward bullies.

"Pio," I said, unbuckling the gun belt, "the law will be along in a few minutes. In the meantime, you see we aren't interrupted."

"Sure, Cap." Pio looked at Jimbo, grinning. "You want to quit now, big fella? You want to quit while you're all in one piece?"

"Why, you damn' fool!" Jimbo said, and came at me.

He was ten years younger than I and sixty pounds heavier, and he was fast. Moreover, somewhere he had boxed a little, stand-up, amateur style. He jabbed and I let it go over my right shoulder and hit him in the ribs with a solid right. It was like hitting the side of a barn.

As my right landed I rolled left and hooked into his belly, then missed with an overhand right for his chin. He rushed into me, clubbing me down, striking for the back of my neck and my kidneys. He had huge fists, great knobs of bone and muscle, and every time he hit he shook me.

I stabbed a left into his mouth, crossed a right for the chin, and then we went at it, toe to toe, punching like crazy men. I was landing two punches to his one, but they seemed to have no effect.

He dove at me suddenly, grabbing me around the legs

118

and jerking them from under me. As I fell, I hooked him in the face, stabbing for his eyes with my thumb.

He didn't like it, and jerked his head away and I jammed the butt of my palm under his chin. For a moment we strained, and then I quickly jerked my hand away and hit him on the Adam's apple. He jerked back, choking and gasping, and I heaved him off.

Before he could get off his knees I slugged him in the face, smashing his lips into a bloody pulp. He came at me then, swinging with both hands. I ducked the first punch, caught the second, and it knocked me back into a table, which crumpled under me. He jumped to put the boots to me but I rolled free and slammed him behind the knees. His knees buckled and he fell, and then we both got up.

I was mad but I was liking it, and before he could get set I stepped in, jabbed a left to the bloody mouth and crossed a right that split the pulpy flesh on his cheek right down to the bone. He butted me under the chin with his head, stamped on my feet, tried to knee me. Jerking up my own knee, I avoided that, then threw him with a rolling hip-lock.

He got up off the floor, his face a great blotch of blood, and I feinted. He waved a hand to try to brush the punch away and I smashed him in the mouth with my right.

He slugged me on the chin and I felt my knees slump. He hit me again, and everything went black. I started to fall, but pushed myself against him. He staggered back, trying to get punching range, and my vision cleared a bit.

I'd never been a day out of shape in my life, and I was glad of it now. I shook my head to clear it, and when he swung a kick at me I caught his foot with mine and swung it high and across, then dove at him while he was poised on one leg. He went down and I landed with my knee in his solar plexus, then smashed it up into his chin.

He threw me off and came up, wiping blood from his face.

He lunged to his feet and I kicked my toe into the nerve centers of his upper thigh. He almost fell, started to step forward, and the leg moved clumsily, still numb from the blow. Moving around him, I feinted, then smashed a right to his chin as he came in.

There was a taste of blood in my mouth, and my brain was foggy from the blows I had taken on the head and chin. He was slow now, but so was I. Sweat trickled into my eyes. He lunged at me suddenly and I sprang back. As I did so, Colin shoved an up-ended chair behind me and I toppled over it to the floor.

Jimbo jumped in the air as I grabbed the chair, planning to come down on me with his heels in my stomach. He came down all right, right into the legs of the chair that I smashed upward at him. The chair caught him in the groin.

He screamed and fell to his knees. Picking up the chair, I broke it over his head and shoulders, and he slid down on the floor and lay there, still.

Tom Riley and two highway policemen stood in the doorway. Apparently they had been standing there for some time, enjoying the fight.

"I hope you didn't kill him," Riley said mildly.

"He's tough," I said, and dropped down on the sofa among the debris.

"Mr. Wells," Riley said, "we'd like you to come into town and answer some questions."

After a moment I got to my feet and went outside. I went to the shower room off the pool and splashed water on my face. It was stiff and sore, and it hurt to the touch. There was a welt under my eye that had turned black, my lip was split, my ear swollen out of shape and there was a lump on my jaw and another over my eye. How my body looked I didn't know. I only knew how it felt. I must have caught a lot of punches I didn't even remember.

"Dan?" It was Belle Dawson.

"I thought I sent you into town?"

"I came back. I had to. I couldn't stand having you out here, not knowing what was happening. So when we met the police car a few miles up the road, I decided to return with them."

"Come on," I said, "we've got something to do."

Pio fell in beside us. "I put the guns down," he said. "The officers know me, and they might misunderstand." He grinned at me. "This is the first time I have done nothing wrong. It is a good feeling."

We picked up the electric lantern Dad Styles had carried and I led the way into the old fort.

Inside, I pushed an old box aside and counted the stones from the back wall. At the third stone I stopped. The stone was about a foot square. With a pick that Pio brought in from outside, I hacked away at the mortar and lifted out the stone. Under it, in the earth under the old fort, was a stone-walled compartment, and in it a rusted iron box.

We broke the box open with the pick. Inside, wrapped in a torn oil-skin slicker, were two squares of tanned buckskin. On one was Indian picture-writing; on the other a legal document in Spanish, signed and sealed.

"John Toomey was a careful man," I said. "He bought the land from the Apaches, and got them to designate the boundaries with care and to describe in their own picture-writing the land sold to him. Then he looked up the man who was the last heir to the Spanish grant and bought him out. Now it's all yours, Belle, or will be when the legal arrangements are completed."

"And where will you be then?"

"I'll likely be a witness, and that will keep me around for a while, but if you have any further ideas on the subject we might cut up a steak some evening and discuss them."

We stood together under the stars then, and I was thinking of the last words that John Toomey had written.

The directions had been there, of course, telling where to find the papers recording the sale of the ranch property to John and Clyde Toomey.

But there was more, the last words written by John Toomey before he stuffed the papers into the gun barrel.

"It is my request that whoever will come upon these pages will seek out those who have done this crime and

show their guilt that the evil may not profit from evil, and that my sons and grandsons may grow tall upon the land I came so far to find."

I'll say one thing for John Toomey: when he loaded that Bisley Colt for the last time, it was really loaded.

ABOUT THE AUTHOR

LOUIS L'AMOUR has written of himself: "My great-grandfather was killed by the Sioux. I've known the famous gunfighters, men who fought in sheep and cattle wars, men who fought the Indians on their own ground.

"The West was wilder than any man can write it, but my facts, my terrain, my guns, my Indians are real. I've ridden and hunted the country. When I write about a spring, that spring is there, and the water is good to drink."

With this background and authority, Louis L'Amour has written over twenty superior novels about the West.

FREE CATALOG
of over 650 Bantam Books

• All The New Releases • Best-Selling Authors • Chilling Mysteries • Thundering Westerns • Startling Science-Fiction • Gripping Novels • Anthologies • Dramas • Reference Books • More.

BANTAM BOOKS
CURRENT CATALOG

This fascinating catalog of Bantam Books contains a complete list of paper-bound editions of best-selling books originally priced from $2.00 to $7.00. Yours now in Bantam editions for just 35¢ to $1.45. Here is your opportunity to read the best-sellers you've missed, and add to your private library at huge savings. The catalog is free! Send for yours today.

Ready for Mailing Now
Send for your FREE copy today

BANTAM BOOKS, INC.

Dept. GA3, 414 East Golf Road, Des Plaines, Ill.

Please send me the new catalog of Bantam Books, containing a complete list of more than 650 editions available to me for as little as 35¢.

Name_____

Address_____

City_____Zone_____State_____